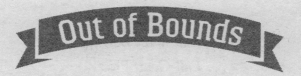

Out of Bounds

Also by Elena Delle Donne

Hoops
Elle of the Ball
Full-Court Press
Digging Deep

My Shot

HOOPS
Out of Bounds

3

Elena Delle Donne

Simon & Schuster Books for Young Readers
New York London Toronto Sydney New Delhi

SIMON & SCHUSTER BOOKS FOR YOUNG READERS
An imprint of Simon & Schuster Children's Publishing Division
1230 Avenue of the Americas, New York, New York 10020
This book is a work of fiction. Any references to historical events, real people, or real places are used fictitiously. Other names, characters, places, and events are products of the author's imagination, and any resemblance to actual events or places or persons, living or dead, is entirely coincidental.
Text copyright © 2018 by Elena Delle Donne
Cover illustrations copyright © 2018 by Cassey Kuo
All rights reserved, including the right of reproduction in whole or in part in any form.
SIMON & SCHUSTER BOOKS FOR YOUNG READERS
is a trademark of Simon & Schuster, Inc.
For information about special discounts for bulk purchases, please contact Simon & Schuster Special Sales at 1-866-506-1949
or business@simonandschuster.com.
The Simon & Schuster Speakers Bureau can bring authors to your live event. For more information or to book an event, contact the Simon & Schuster Speakers Bureau at 1-866-248-3049 or visit our website at www.simonspeakers.com.
Also available in a Simon & Schuster Books for Young Readers hardcover edition
Cover design by Laurent Linn
Interior design by Hilary Zarycky
The text for this book was set in Minister.
Manufactured in the United States of America
1119 OFF
First Simon & Schuster Books for Young Readers paperback edition December 2019
2 4 6 8 10 9 7 5 3 1
The Library of Congress has cataloged the hardcover edition as follows:
Names: Delle Donne, Elena, author.
Title: Out of bounds / Elena Delle Donne.
Description: First edition. | New York : Simon & Schuster Books for Young Readers, [2018] | Series: Hoops ; 3 | Summary: Elle begins to question whether basketball is worth the time and effort she is putting in, and who she would be if not a basketball star.
Identifiers: LCCN 2018013352| ISBN 9781534412378 (hardback) |
ISBN 9781534412385 (pbk) ISBN 9781534412392 (eBook)
Subjects: | CYAC: Basketball—Fiction. | Self-Confidence—Fiction. | Middle schools—Fiction. | Schools—Fiction. | BISAC: JUVENILE FICTION / Sports & Recreation / Basketball. | JUVENILE FICTION / Girls & Women. | JUVENILE FICTION / Social Issues / Self-Esteem & Self-Reliance.
Classification: LCC PZ7.1.D4558 Out 2018 | DDC [Fic]—dc23 LC record available at https://lccn.loc.gov/2018013352

To Gia

Acknowledgments

I have a team of people that I would like to thank, and I fully recognize that I would not be where I am today without the support of my family and friends behind me.

Amanda, my wife and my best friend, you have given up and sacrificed so much to help me better my career (even being my off-season workout partner). Words cannot express how much you mean to me, and I am so excited that you are with me for life. We are a pretty unstoppable team.

Special thanks to my incredible parents, who have been with me since day one. Mom, thank you for being extremely honest, absolutely hilarious, and my ultimate role model for what strength looks like.

Dad, thank you for driving me all the way to Pennsylvania twice a week, attending every AAU tournament, and still traveling to lots of my WNBA games. You are my biggest fan.

To my older sister, Lizzie, thank you for helping me keep everything in perspective. You remind me that there is so much more to life, and that joys can come from anywhere—even something as simple as the wind or a perfectly cooked rib eye. You are the greatest gift to our family. And thanks to my big brother, Gene, for being able to make me laugh, especially through the lows, and for being my biggest cheerleader.

Wrigley, my greatest friend and Greatest Dane. Thanks for being my rock in Chicago and for attacking me with love every time I come home. Rasta, thanks for being the edge and sass in our home and for being the only one in our house who can keep Amanda in check.

Erin Kane and Alyssa Romano, thank you for helping me discover myself and for helping me find my voice. This wouldn't have happened without the greatest team behind me.

Thanks to my Octagon literary agent, Jennifer Keene, for all her great work on this project. Thanks to the all-stars at Simon & Schuster, including Liz Kossnar.

Thank you all.

Out of Bounds

It's All About Pressure

Reminder: You have basketball practice starting at 3:15, Elle!

The message appeared on my cell phone screen when the last school bell of the day rang. Normally I wouldn't need a reminder to go to basketball practice. There was no way I could forget that I had practice with my seventh-grade team, the Spring Meadow Nighthawks, every Monday, Wednesday, and Friday after school, plus a game every Sunday. Basketball has been my life ever since third grade.

But the reason why my phone *was* reminding me

was because my best friend, Avery, had just down-loaded a scheduling program for me. She'd just presented it to me a few hours ago during lunch in the cafeteria. And if it sounds strange that my best friend was scheduling my life for me, there's a pretty good reason.

Recently I almost had a meltdown because of all the things I was busy with: basketball, my new dog, volunteering, homework, helping my family, and hanging with friends. I had been getting bad grades, hurting my friends' feelings, and psyching myself out on the court because I couldn't figure out how to prioritize my time.

Avery's app looked like it was going to fix all that. And I owed my teammates on the Nighthawks a big thanks, too, because they had all offered to take vol-unteer slots at Camp Cooperation—an after-school program for kids with special needs. I had been vol-unteering there twice a week, but since my friends were helping out, I could cut down my days to two Tuesdays a month and free up time for the other things in my life.

Today was Monday, and like the app said, I had basketball practice. We practice in the high school gym, which is just a short walk across a field from the middle school. That's because the school I go to, Spring Meadow School, is a small, private school. It's a K–12 school and there are three buildings on our campus: one for kids in K–5, one for kids in grades 6–8, and one for the high school.

I'd been wanting to thank my teammates since Avery had told me the news at lunchtime. As we walked across the field together, I had my chance.

"I want to thank you guys for volunteering at Camp Cooperation," I said.

"I had fun the day we all volunteered as a team," Natalie said. "Those kids are cute."

"Especially your brother Pete, Caroline," Dina remarked.

Caroline's brother Pete is eight years old and has Down syndrome. She and I recently bonded because I have a special needs sister too. But my sister, Beth, is older than I am, and she has different conditions than Pete does.

"He's cute if you only have to spend an hour a week with him," Caroline joked. "But I am really glad that everyone on the team is going to take turns. I know Pete really loves the program—all the kids do."

Walking in front of me were two of our best players, Bianca and Tiff.

"Yeah, Avery told us you needed help organizing your schedule," Bianca said snidely. "Now maybe you can concentrate on your game."

I ignored the comment. Bianca is one of the tallest players on the team, but she's still six inches shorter than I am (I'm six foot). At the start of the season, Coach Ramirez made me center and that really upset Bianca. She's been calling me out ever since.

Tiff is Bianca's best friend, but she's been a little bit nicer.

"I told Avery that I'd help you study for science," Tiff said.

"Yeah, she told me," I replied. "That would be great. Cellular biology is kicking my butt."

Tiff grinned. "Then we will kick its butt together!"

We had reached the high school gym and headed for the locker room. I changed into my practice uniform and laced up my basketball shoes. I'd had to get new ones after my feet literally grew two sizes over the summer, which was probably the only thing I liked about my growth spurt. I am obsessed with basketball shoes and I would buy a new pair every month if I could afford to.

Then I looked in the mirror and pulled my long blond hair into a ponytail. I took a deep breath. Coach Ramirez started each practice with a video review of our last game. Yesterday we'd had a game against the Patriots, and I had choked. For the first time in my entire basketball career, I hadn't scored. I'd even missed a lousy free throw shot—usually my specialty! So I was expecting Coach Ramirez to be extra hard on me.

When we entered the gym, Coach was pacing back and forth in front of the bleachers. On a normal day she looks like she means business, without a strand of her short brown hair out of place, and a

Nighthawks T-shirt that always looks freshly ironed. Today she looked even more serious than ever, her mouth set in a thin line.

"Losing is one thing," she began right off the bat. "Sometimes we lose even though we played our best. But we did *not* play our best."

She hit a button on the keyboard and the game began to play from the start. I was in the middle of the court facing the Patriots center, who was almost six foot tall, maybe an inch shorter than I was. We both jumped up for the ball, and she tipped it before I could.

"You could have had that, Elle!" Coach said. "You're my center. I need you to be hungrier for that ball."

I nodded. I was getting kind of used to Coach singling me out in the reviews by now, so it didn't sting quite as bad. But it still hurt.

Coach's next comment was directed toward Patrice—her daughter, and our starting small forward.

"Patrice, you had a shot there, and you didn't

take it!" she barked. "You need more confidence out there."

Patrice nodded and looked down at her shoes.

How can she be confident when her mom is always pointing out her mistakes? I wondered.

Coach fast-forwarded through the video, stopping in a few places. Some of her comments were general—we needed to be blocking more shots; we had to be careful not to travel with the ball. But I felt like she made comments about me more than anyone else (except maybe Patrice). I just kept hearing, "Elle! You lost focus there." "Elle! That was sloppy footwork." "Elle! You could have taken a shot there."

I glanced over at Avery and she gave me a sympathetic look. She knew that I hated Video Mondays.

Finally we finished the review.

"Everyone on this team has problems traveling," Coach said. "So today we're going to do some control drills."

We had never done control drills before, so I was curious to see what Coach had in mind. First she had us all line up on one side of the court.

"All right, now stand with your right foot forward, in shooting position," she instructed, and we all obeyed. (Natalie, who's left-handed, stood with her left foot forward.)

"Now we're going to play a game of Stop and Go," Coach continued. "When I say 'go,' run forward. When I say 'stop,' stop and return to shooting position."

We did this several times back and forth across the gym. It wasn't always easy to stop with my right foot forward, so I could see why the drill was a good idea. After we did that a few times, Coach changed things up. This time we dribbled while we ran, stopped in shooting position, and then started again. First Coach had us do it slowly, and then faster.

After the control drills, Coach called for a scrimmage.

"Oh great," I said to Avery. "What if I can't score again? Maybe I'm cursed and my scoring days are over."

"Stop psyching yourself out, Elle!" Avery told me. "You're a great shooter and you know it."

Coach divided us up into two teams for the

scrimmage: Me, Avery, Dina, Hannah, and Caroline on one team, and Bianca, Tiff, Amanda, Patrice, and Natalie on the other.

Bianca and I faced each other as center, and when Coach threw the ball up, I jumped as high and hard as I could. I was not going to give Bianca the satisfaction of getting it. Not today.

I tipped the ball to Dina, who pivoted and passed it to Hannah. Hannah dribbled forward a few steps and then stopped and made her shot. It bounced off the rim, but I caught the rebound and sank the ball for two points.

I grinned at Avery. Making the shot was a huge relief! I felt energized, and I had fun with the scrimmage. But Bianca was on fire, too, and her team ended up beating us by two points.

"Great scrimmage!" Coach complimented us as we cooled off from the game. "Now let's go over the Thanksgiving schedule again. Don't forget that we don't have a regular practice on Wednesday, the half day. We'll be meeting outside on the field for a team-building activity. Lunch is on me. Then there's no practice on Friday, and no game on Sunday."

The thought of a break from practice and competition cheered me up—although I was a little afraid of what Coach's idea of a team-building activity would turn out to be. In elementary school, we'd done stuff like make towers out of marshmallows and toothpicks. I couldn't imagine Coach Ramirez doing anything that silly.

We all grabbed our duffel bags from the locker room and made our way through the high school halls to the main entrance, where our parents would come to get us. Just about everyone was talking about their Thanksgiving plans.

"There's a lot of yellow on your U-Plan schedule this weekend," Avery told me. "I hope I can come over and meet Zobe finally."

Zobe is my almost-brand-new dog, a Great Dane my family adopted from the local shelter. Avery had been dying to meet him, but I'd kept putting her off because I was so busy.

"Yes, yes, yes!" I said.

"Great! I'll send you a U-Plan request, and if

you approve, it will automatically upload into your schedule," she said.

"I have no idea what you just said, but it sounds good," I replied.

Amanda, who'd just started playing basketball this year, chimed in. "I would love to go on another doggy date with Freckles and Zobe, but we're going to my grandmother's this weekend in Pennsylvania."

Freckles is an English springer spaniel with cute freckles, just like Amanda. I was just starting to get to know Amanda, and we'd had some great walks and talks in the park with our dogs.

"Is Freckles going with you, or do you have to put her in a kennel?" I asked.

"Grandma loves dogs, so Freckles is allowed to come with us," she replied.

"That's nice," I said. "We've got our family coming over this Thanksgiving, so we don't have to travel anywhere. I wonder how Zobe's going to be with a lot of people in the house, though. He's a pretty good dog, but we haven't started his obedience training classes yet."

"He'll be fine," Amanda assured me with a smile. "He's a big sweetheart."

Bianca, Tiffany, and Dina were walking behind us, talking with one another, and right at that moment, Bianca's voice got really loud.

"It's about time Coach let me play center already," she was saying.

Normally I would have ignored her. And I might not have argued with her, because I had been a shooting guard in the past and hadn't even wanted to be center when Coach gave me the position. But now I was the center, whether I liked it or not, and I was tired of Bianca giving me a hard time about it.

I turned around. "Bianca, can't you just give me a chance, please?" I asked. "The season just started, and the pressure you're giving me just isn't helping."

Bianca rolled her eyes. "If you can't take the pressure, Elle, then you shouldn't be center," she said. "That's the whole point. It's all about pressure."

Then the three of them walked past us.

Avery shook her head. "I do not understand what her problem is."

"I think she really loves the game more than any-thing," Natalie said. "That's why she works so hard, and why she cares about how everybody else on the team is performing."

"Good point," Hannah said. "I'm glad she's on our team, and not on anybody else's."

I didn't chime in. I was replaying Natalie's words in my head.

She really loves this game more than anything.

That was sure true about Bianca. But was it true about me? Did I love basketball more than *anything*?

And if I didn't . . . well, what did that mean?

Dad's Vision of the Future

The next day I got a ride home from school with my other best friend, Blake. His mom, Mrs. Tanaka, picked us up.

I've known Blake even longer than I've known Avery. The Tanakas lived next door to us in Greenmont, Delaware. It's a small town near Wilmington, where Spring Meadow School is. Blake and I were born four months apart, and our moms brought us together for lots of baby playdates. We've been friends ever since, and not just because of our history, but because we have a lot in common. For one thing, we both love basketball. Blake plays on the seventh-grade boys' team.

"Want to play some one-on-one when we get home?" Blake asked.

"Sure," I said, and then I remembered my app. "Wait, hold on."

I checked my phone.

3:30: *Walk Zobe.*

4:00–5:30: *Homework*

"Um, I can't," I said. "I have to work on my history project. But you can walk Zobe with me if you want. I need to do that first."

Blake shrugged. "Sure," he said, and then he glanced at my phone. "What's that? Some kind of scheduling app?"

I nodded. "Yeah, Avery downloaded it for me."

"Does this mean you won't have time to play basketball with your best friend Blake?" he asked.

"Of course not!" I said. "It's just supposed to keep me on track so I don't let important things slide. I have lots of free time this weekend, see?"

Mrs. Tanaka piped up. "That sounds like a very

sensible idea, Elle. You should get that app, Blake."

Blake looked at me and rolled his eyes. *Thanks a lot,* he mouthed, and I tried not to laugh.

"Plus, you're coming over for Thanksgiving, right?" I asked. "You know we always end up playing a game of pickup then. It's tradition!"

"Yeah," he said. "Maybe this year we can finally beat Jim and your dad."

"I am looking forward to Thanksgiving," Mrs. Tanaka said. "Your mother makes the most delicious roasted squash."

"And I love your wasabi deviled eggs," I said.

Mrs. Tanaka smiled into the rearview mirror. "They're my specialty. I'm glad you like them."

The car pulled into the Tanakas' driveway.

"I'll meet you and Zobe back here in a minute," Blake said.

Blake went inside his house to dump his backpack, and I walked through the front door of my house. Normally I'd find Mom and Beth in the kitchen at this time of day, but they weren't there.

"Hello?" I called out.

"We're out back!" Mom replied.

I followed her voice to the backyard and found Mom and Beth playing catch with Zobe. When he saw me, he came running and almost knocked me down!

"Easy there, Zobe!" I told him.

Zobe is a big dog—male Great Danes can grow to almost three feet tall and weigh as much as two hundred pounds! So when he jumps on you, it's almost like being tackled by a short football player.

"Beth kept tracing 'dog' and 'outside,'" Mom told me. "She really loves playing catch with him."

I walked over to Beth, who was sitting in her wheelchair, and knelt down so she could sniff my head. Beth is deaf and blind, and has cerebral palsy and autism. So she recognizes people by their smell.

Then she took my hand and traced two symbols onto it with her fingers. Beth communicates with a form of sign language that's unique to her because regular sign language is too complicated.

Dog happy, she said.

Love, I replied.

Then I looked at Mom. "I need to take Zobe for his walk, but I hate to take him away from Beth."

"We've been playing for a while, Elle," Mom said. "I'll let her know that we're going back inside."

I kissed Beth's forehead and then put Zobe on his leash.

"Be back in thirty minutes!" I called to Mom.

Blake was waiting for me in front of the house, and we talked as we walked Zobe down the streets of Greenmont.

"Heard you had a rough game yesterday," Blake said.

"Yeah, it was brutal," I said. "I didn't even score. Not once."

Blake's eyes got wide. "You? Elle Deluca? The scoring wizard of Spring Meadow?"

"Not anymore," I said, and I kicked a rock on the path in front of me.

"Don't let it get to you," Blake said. "Everybody has bad games. Even the pros."

I sighed. "Yeah, that's what my dad said. But I'm starting to think I'm not meant to play basketball."

"Wait. Seriously, Elle?" Blake asked. "I mean, you've been playing ever since I can remember. You're the perfect height. It's like you were born to play."

"But what if I was born to do something else?" I asked him.

"Like what?" Blake shot back.

I thought about that. I loved Zobe. Maybe I could be a vet. And I loved volunteering at Camp Cooperation. Maybe one day I could run a program like that. Or maybe I was good at something else I hadn't even tried yet.

"I'm not sure," I said. "But we should get back. I need to start on my history project."

When I got back home, I went right to my room and got to work on my project for World History. It's my favorite subject, but I had been weirdly stressed out about it because I didn't have time to work on the project before Avery's help with the app. But that day, as I sat at my desk and read about ancient African civilizations on my laptop and took notes, I found myself completely absorbed. Before I knew it,

Mom was calling me to set the dinner table, and I had gotten a lot of work done.

I set five places at the table because now that football season was over, my brother, Jim, didn't have practice every night and he could eat with us.

"Grandma and Grandpa will be here tomorrow night," Mom announced as we sat down to plates of meatloaf, mashed potatoes, and green beans. "Elle, I need you to sleep on the cot in the basement and give them your room."

"No problem," I replied. The basement is a cozy family room with a fuzzy carpet, a TV, and two couches. It's actually kind of fun sleeping down there.

"And I need both of you to help with cleaning up tomorrow," Mom said.

"Sure," I said. "But right after school the basketball team is doing a team-building thing."

"Oh, right," Mom said. "I forgot about that."

"I didn't. Coach reminded us today," I replied. Then I held up my phone. "Also, it's in my awesome new schedule."

Mom smiled. "It was so sweet of Avery to do that for you. And to coordinate with us so she could surprise you."

"It was," I said, and I turned to Dad. "I'm excited to take Zobe to obedience class with you. Thanks for setting that up."

Jim looked up from his plate. "Obedience? It's about time. That dog dumped out my whole laundry bag yesterday. My floor was covered with socks and underwear."

"How is that different than any other day?" I teased.

"Back to tomorrow," Mom said. "What time is your team building over, Elle? I'm supposed to pick up the pies in the early afternoon."

She looked at my dad. "Can you pick her up, Eddie?"

"I can bring Elle home," Jim said. "Some guys from the team are going out to lunch tomorrow in Wilmington. I'll get her on my way back."

Mom sighed. "It's still hard to believe that your last football season is over."

"It won't be his last," Dad said. "We'll be going to all of Jim's college games."

Jim frowned. "That's if I get on a team."

"Don't worry about that, Jim," Dad said. "We've already got three meetings with recruiters set up after Thanksgiving."

"Really?" I asked. "When did this happen?"

Jim shrugged. "They started to call during the season. And one came to that last game."

"Wow!" I said. "That's exciting!"

Then I thought of something. "If you play college football, does that mean you'll go pro?"

"I haven't thought that far ahead yet," Jim said. "I mean, sometimes I dream about going pro, you know? Then other times I'm not sure."

I nodded. I knew exactly what he meant.

"We may end up with two pros in this family," Dad said. "One NFL star, and one WNBA star. We might have to buy an RV so we can travel to all your games."

He got a dreamy look in his eyes. "I can see it now. Me and your mom and Beth sitting in a glass box in the stadium, watching our kids from the best seats in the house and cheering them on."

I started to drag my fork around in my mashed potatoes. Dad seemed so excited about us both becoming pro athletes. . . . Would it crush him if I decided not to go pro one day?

Luckily Mom started talking about Thanksgiving and everyone who was coming, and Dad dropped the subject. I finished my plate, helped clean up, and then realized I actually had free time before bed. I spent it by scrolling through pages of basketball shoes online. No matter how I felt about playing basketball, I didn't think my basketball shoe obsession would ever end!

The Turkey Games

All right, girls!" Coach Ramirez announced the next day. "It's time for the Turkey Games to begin!"

"The Turkey Games?" Avery whispered to me, and I answered with a shrug. I had no idea what to expect. We were outside on a cool but sunny fall day, standing on the school field. Scattered on the grass were a variety of strange objects: Hula-Hoops, beach balls, and pool noodles. Coach smiled when she saw us looking at them.

"We're going to have a little fun today," Coach

said. "The Turkey Games are a tradition for my teams. They are a series of games that have no serious purpose whatsoever. But first, I must ask you all a *very* serious question."

She paused dramatically. "If you could only eat one food for the rest of your life, what would it be? Pizza or burgers?"

Natalie raised her hand. "What if you don't like pizza *or* burgers?"

"You have to pick one," Coach said. "Think outside the box. It could be dessert pizza. Or a veggie burger. But you have to pick one. When you're ready, go over there if you choose pizza." She pointed to her left. "And over there if you choose burgers."

I walked to the left, because while I love burgers I was pretty sure I couldn't live without eating another slice of pizza. Tiff, Bianca, Amanda, and Natalie all chose pizza too. Avery, Patrice, Hannah, Dina, and Caroline chose burgers.

"Perfect!" Coach said. "Now we have two teams. You have sixty seconds to give your team a name."

I looked over at Avery. "Burgers? Really?" I called out.

"I like veggie burgers!" she replied.

"Elle, let's focus," Bianca said. "We need to come up with a name."

"How about the Pizza Pals?" Amanda suggested.

"I don't know. The word 'pals' is kind of lame," Bianca said.

I jumped to Amanda's defense. "Well, I like it," I said.

"How about the Cheese Champions?" Natalie suggested.

"I think I like Pizza Pals better," Tiff said.

"Ten seconds!" Coach called out.

Bianca frowned. "Come on, there's got to be something better. I don't know, maybe the Pepperoni—"

"Time's up!" Coach yelled. "Pizza lovers, what's your team name?"

"The Pizza Pals!" Tiff replied.

"And we're the Burger Squad!" Dina called out.

"Okay, Burger Squad and Pizza Pals, please line up on the same side of the field," Coach said. "It's time for our first event: the beach ball relay races!"

Then she explained the rules. Each member of the team had to use a pool noodle to push a beach ball down the field to a cone, then come back to the team to return the ball to the next in line. Coach demonstrated, making it look easy.

"Elle, you go first, and I'll go last to make up for any lost time," Bianca said confidently. She had taken the role of the Pizza Pals team leader, but I didn't mind so much. I'd known Bianca since first grade and she had always been like that, and it wasn't a big deal. But lately she'd been calling me out in a mean way, and that was starting to get on my nerves.

Today was supposed to be team building, so I figured I'd let Bianca boss me around if she wanted to. I took my place at the head of the line and glanced over at Avery, who was up first for the Burger Squad.

"You are going down!" I taunted her.

"No way!" Avery countered.

Coach Ramirez started a countdown. "On your mark, get set, go!"

I whacked the beach ball with my pool noodle, and it skidded wildly toward the edge of the field. As I raced after it, I could hear my team cheering me on behind me.

When I caught up to it, I didn't hit it so hard this time. I carefully made my way back onto the course and tried to catch up with Avery. She reached the cone before I did, but she lost control of the beach ball as she made the turn. I was being extra careful so I made the turn smoothly.

"Oh no, you don't!" Avery yelled, and she quickly caught up with me. Breathless and laughing, we reached our teams at the same time. I handed the pool noodle to Amanda.

"Don't hit it too hard," I warned her, but I was too late—she whacked it just like I did and the ball went flying and bounced off Dina's head on the other team.

"Whoops! Sorry!" Amanda cried. She grabbed the ball and got back into the race.

"I call foul!" Dina joked.

Amanda's wild ball put her behind Patrice, and

then Dina took off like a rocket for the Burger Squad. By the time Bianca came up, the Burger Squad's last racer, Caroline, had already reached the cone.

With her mouth set in a determined line, Bianca raced to the cone, moving the beach ball along with such skill that I would have sworn she had practiced doing it. She got to the cone really quickly and made a perfect turn. She was right on Caroline's heels, but Caroline reached the Burger Squad first.

"And the Burger Squad wins!" Coach Ramirez announced.

The Burger Squad cheered. Bianca's face clouded and she kicked the grass.

"Rats!" she muttered.

"Aw, come on, B, it's just for fun," Tiff told her, but Bianca didn't respond. It got me thinking about what Natalie and Hannah had said the other day—about how much Bianca liked to win. I was starting to realize how competitive she really was.

Coach Ramirez held up two Hula-Hoops.

"Okay, now I need each team to form a circle," she said.

We obeyed, and Coach put one Hula-Hoop on Tiff's arm and one on Hannah's arm.

"All right, now I need everybody to hold hands," she instructed.

I grabbed Amanda's hand with my left hand, and Natalie's hand with my right.

"So, the object of this game is to pass the Hula-Hoop around the circle without letting go of your hands," Coach explained.

"How are we supposed to do that?" Natalie asked.

Coach grinned. "I'm sure you'll figure it out. Ready, set, go!"

We were lucky that Coach had started with Tiff, because she figured it out quickly. She shrugged her shoulder and put the Hula-Hoop over her head. Then she let it drop and stepped through it so that it dropped onto her other arm.

"Your turn, Bianca!" she said.

Bianca had figured it out, too, and did it expertly, passing it to Caroline. Caroline stepped through the hoop and passed it to Natalie.

"We've got this!" Bianca cheered. "Hurry!"

Natalie stepped through the hoop, and then passed the hoop to me. I put my head through it and let it drop, and then I stuck my foot through it, and then my other foot—and then I fell flat on my face, taking the team down with me!

We tumbled onto the grass. I'd tripped because I still hadn't quite figured out how to control my extra-long legs yet.

Everyone was laughing—except for Bianca.

"Elle, no!" she wailed.

Then Coach's voice rang out. "The Burger Squad wins!"

Our friends on the Burger Squad cheered. Bianca rolled her eyes.

"Figured I would get stuck on a team with the giant klutz," she muttered, but of course I heard it. We all did.

"Bianca, loosen up. It's just a game," Tiff said, but Bianca just glared at her.

"Okay, now we're moving on to a new game called Zombie," Coach Ramirez announced. "We're going to need three teams for this one, so the Pizza Pals and Burger Squad need to disband."

"Wait, what?" Bianca blurted out. "Can't we do best of five or something?"

"Lunch is on the way," Coach replied. "And I want to get a game of Zombie in. It's a lot of fun."

Bianca frowned.

"Caroline, Dina, Amanda, Avery, Natalie, you're zombies," Coach said, pointing. "Elle, Tiff, Hannah, you're survivors. Bianca and Patrice, you're helpers."

Then she explained the rules. The goal of the game was for the survivors to make it to the far end of the field without being tagged by a zombie. For one minute, they would be chased by the five zombies. Then the helpers would come in. Helpers couldn't be tagged by zombies, but they could distract the zombies or protect the survivors by surrounding them.

My heart started to beat a little faster as Coach explained things to us. I think the idea of being chased kicked my fight-or-flight system into high gear.

"Ready, set, go!"

Me, Tiff, and Hannah tore onto the field and

charged toward the home base. But that was the zombie starting point, and they came running right for us. I knew we'd have to run in circles first to clear a path to safety.

With five zombies and three survivors, I knew it would be tough to avoid getting tagged. So I ran all the way down the field, opposite home base, and hoped the zombies would focus on Tiff and Hannah. Some of them did, but Avery was making a beeline right toward me.

As she got close, I faked right and made my way to the far left side of the field. At that point I saw Bianca and Patrice run onto the field. Our helpers had arrived!

I was just a few feet away from them, and I expected them to help me with Avery, but they seemed to have a mission. First they ran toward Tiff and then made a circle around her, holding hands. Natalie and Amanda tried to break through to get Tiff, but Bianca and Patrice got her safely to home base.

That left me and Hannah as the only survivors. Bianca and Patrice caught up to Hannah and used the same technique on her. That kept zombie Dina and zombie Caroline busy, but it sent Natalie and Amanda running toward me.

"Heeeeeeeelp!" I wailed. Now I had three zombies after me! I zigzagged across the field while they chased me, laughing. Where were Bianca and Patrice? I needed them.

I made it about three-quarters of the way to home base when the zombies cornered me. Avery, Amanda, and Natalie all tagged me, and I groaned.

"Mmm, delicious brains," Natalie said.

"Yay! Elle's a zombie now, just like us!" Amanda cheered.

Coach's whistle blew. "Zombies win!"

"Wait, you mean there was a winner to this game?" Bianca asked.

"If all the survivors make it safely to base, survivors and helpers win," Coach said. "If they don't, the zombies win."

"Oh," Bianca said. "You didn't say that in the beginning."

Right then I understood what had happened.

Bianca must have purposely not helped me (I didn't blame Patrice, who was probably just doing what Bianca had told her). She thought *I* would lose, and didn't realize she would lose too. Ha!

At that moment, two delivery guys appeared—one holding three pizza boxes and another holding two large paper bags from Burger Shack.

"Lunch is here!" Coach announced. "Go inside and wash up. We'll eat out here at the picnic tables."

A few minutes later we were all sitting outside the high school building, eating pizza and burgers and laughing about the team-building exercises.

"I can't believe how hard it was to move a beach ball with a pool noodle," Hannah remarked.

"And I can't believe that I fell on my face during the Hula-Hoop challenge and took everyone down with me," I said. "Sorry about that."

"It's okay, it was fun," Amanda said, and the rest of the Pizza Pals nodded except for Bianca, who scowled.

Honestly, it was annoying, but I didn't let it get to me. Hanging out with the team was a lot of fun—

maybe my favorite part of playing basketball. Here on the field, with the bright blue sky overhead, eating pizza and burgers, there was no pressure at all. No pressure to perform well or make baskets. Just fun.

Then I remembered that we had no game on Sunday, and I smiled. I was ready for a pressure-free holiday weekend!

Zobe, No!

I woke up Thanksgiving morning to Zobe licking my face. I slowly opened my eyes, confused for a second about why I wasn't seeing any WNBA posters. Then I remembered that I was sleeping in the basement.

"Good morning, Zobe," I said with a yawn. "What time is it?"

Zobe answered me with a whine, so I picked up my phone from the floor next to the cot I had slept on. It was 7:15—a half hour later than when I usually wake up on a regular school day. Zobe was probably hungry.

"Come on, let's go upstairs," I said.

Still in my pajamas (flannel bottoms and a Nighthawks T-shirt), I headed up into the kitchen with Zobe. Mom was already chopping vegetables at the kitchen island, even though it was early in the morning for that, and Grandma and Grandpa were seated at the table, drinking coffee. They had both arrived the night before, and we had all stayed up late talking. I love when they visit! I walked over and gave them each a hug.

"Good morning, Elle! You're up early for someone who's almost a teenager," Grandma said.

"Zobe needs to go out," I said, moving to open the back door for him. "And I've got to feed him."

I waited until Zobe did his business, and after I cleaned it up, I came back inside with Zobe and washed my hands.

"After breakfast, maybe you can help me peel potatoes," Mom said. "I didn't prep as much as I wanted to yesterday, and there's so much to do!"

Grandpa patted the seat next to him. "Come eat something, Elle. I went to that bakery in Wilmington at six a.m. to get us the crumb cake. What a line! And it's not even as good as the crumb cake at Vitelli's back home."

"It's excellent crumb cake," Grandma said. "You just think nothing can be as good anywhere as it is in Philly."

"Well, that is just a fact," Grandpa said. "You can't argue with facts."

I listened to them bicker as I filled Zobe's bowl with kibble and then poured myself a glass of milk. Grandma and Grandpa are my mom's parents, who live in Philadelphia and have always lived there. Grandma wants to move to Delaware, because she hates the traffic between our house and Philly, but Grandpa doesn't want to move. And whenever they come to our house, they always argue about it.

I sat down and took a piece of crumb cake from the bakery box. Normally the Delucas are a protein/fruit-and-healthy-carb family, especially at break-fast, because Jim and I are athletes and Mom and Dad work out. We'd never eat cake or doughnuts for breakfast, but Grandpa always insists on it whenever he comes to visit. And since crumb cake is delicious, I don't ever complain about it.

"Did you sleep all right downstairs, Elle?" Grandma wanted to know. She's got blond hair like my mom, only she cuts it in short layers. Grandpa has dark brown hair and eyes, so I guess me and my mom both take after Grandma.

"Yeah," I replied, "but the cot is too small for both me and Zobe, and I don't think he liked sleeping on the floor."

Grandma called Zobe over to her and started scratching his head. "He's such a big boy! He must take up a lot of room in your bed."

"He's like a big teddy bear," I said. "And he doesn't move around a lot, so he doesn't wake me up during the night."

Zobe walked away from Grandma and over to the island, where he started sniffing the food that Mom was preparing.

"This is not for you, Zobe," Mom said. "Elle, I need you to keep an eye out on Zobe for me today.

Make sure he stays away from the food and doesn't jump on anybody."

Grandma laughed. "Oh my. I think he's probably as big as Michael and Olivia," she said.

Michael and Olivia are my seven-year-old twin cousins, my Aunt Jess and Uncle Danny's kids. Uncle Danny is my dad's younger brother. They live in Wilmington, and we spend just about every holiday with them.

"I'll make sure Zobe behaves," I promised.

Mom looked over at Grandma and Grandpa. "Next week Elle and Eddie are going to start taking Zobe to obedience classes," she said. "But he hasn't had any training yet."

"He's going to do great," I said. "Aren't you, Zobe?"

At the sound of my voice Zobe bounded over to me, stumbled on his own big feet, and skidded into the table. It shook, and Grandma had to quickly pick up her cup of coffee before it spilled.

"Whoa, Zobe!" I said. "I guess I really can't let you out of my sight today!"

"Take him for a walk after you get dressed, Elle," Mom said, "so he can work off some energy. Then you can help me with the potatoes."

"Sure, Mom," I replied.

The rest of the morning went by really fast. I walked Zobe. I peeled potatoes. I chopped carrots. I set the big table in the living room. I changed into my "nice" clothes, a clean pair of jeans and a blue shirt with a collar (Mom had given up trying to make me get super dressed up on Thanksgiving.)

And then, all at once, the house was full of people. Mr. and Mrs. Tanaka came with Blake. Jim walked in after picking up his girlfriend, Alyssa.

Uncle Danny and Aunt Jess came in right after them, and the twins screamed with excitement when they saw Zobe.

"Elle, you got so tall!" Aunt Jess said, giving me a hug.

"Yup," I answered. People have said that so much to me over the last two months that I'm kind of over it. But Aunt Jess is really nice, so I didn't let it bother me too much.

Then I noticed that Zobe was trying to get his paws up on my cousin Michael.

"Be right back," I said, and I ran to calm down Zobe.

"Elle, he's so big!" Olivia squealed.

"Can I ride him?" Michael asked.

I laughed. "Absolutely not! Zobe is not a horse," I said. "In a little while we can go outside and play with him. But maybe leave him alone right now because he's getting too excited. Okay?"

"Okay," the twins said at the same time, nodding their heads. They both had sandy brown hair and freckles that reminded me of my friend Amanda.

Then Dad called to me from the kitchen. "Elle, can you please help me with this stuff?"

"Sure, Dad," I said, and I left Zobe with the twins and ran to the kitchen. Dad had a platter of cut-up veggies in one hand and a platter of cheese on the other. He nodded to a basket of crackers and a bowl of ranch dip on the counter. "Let's bring all this into the dining room," he said.

I helped Dad carry the appetizers out of the

kitchen, and Mrs. Tanaka walked up to us holding a big platter shaped like a turkey, with deviled eggs arranged on it. Dad's eyes lit up.

"My favorite, Misako! Thank you!" Dad said.

Mrs. Tanaka gave him a big smile. "I know how you and Elle love them, Eddie."

We set up the food on the buffet table in the dining room, and then I heard more squeals from my cousins.

"Zobe! Zobe!"

Michael and Olivia came running past me in the dining room, Zobe at their heels. He chased them into the living room.

"Zobe, no!" I yelled.

I ran after him. "Blake, help!" I called out, because Blake was closer to Zobe than I was.

Blake looked at me, confused, and I bumped into him as I ran to catch up to Zobe. He realized what was happening and the two of us charged after my dog.

"Zobe, stop!" I yelled.

Zobe stopped—but not because I told him to.

He stopped and put his paws on the kitchen island to get another look at the food. His big nose pushed into a bowl of cranberry sauce, and it crashed to the floor.

"Zobe!" I scolded him. I grabbed onto his collar. "Blake, can you please go outside with him? I need to clean this up."

Mom, who had been busy stirring something on the stove, shook her head. "I'll get Jim to clean this up, Elle. You go outside with Zobe and keep him there for a while," she said. "Your dad can set up the gate. Zobe's going to spend the rest of the day downstairs."

I looked at my little cousins. "Come on," I said. "I'll show you how to play fetch with Zobe."

Blake and I brought Michael and Olivia outside and kept them—and Zobe—busy for as long as we could. Then I brought Zobe back in and led him down to the basement.

"You need to hang out here for a while, Zobe," I told him. He climbed up on the couch, put his head on his paws, and looked at me with big, sad eyes. It wasn't easy to leave him that way, but I patted his head and then went back up to the kitchen, closing the doggy gate behind me.

"Sorry about that, Mom," I told her.

"It's all right, Elle," she said. "Jim ran out and bought some more cans of cranberry sauce. But I have to say, I'm glad Zobe will be starting obedience training soon."

"Me too," I agreed, and I hugged her. "Thanks for understanding."

That's my mom, though. When things go wrong, she doesn't freak out. I really admire that about her. I mean, I think I'm pretty chill, too, but nobody beats my mom.

Soon it was time for the main meal, and we all sat around the big dining room table. I rolled Beth's wheelchair so that she was sitting next to Grandma, who is one of her favorite people ever. When Beth was little, before I was born, Grandma spent almost every day with her, and they always bond when Grandma and Grandpa visit.

Grandpa said grace, and then we dug into all

the food: turkey, stuffing, mashed potatoes, glazed carrots, sweet potatoes, Brussels sprouts, cranberry sauce, and two pans of Dad's amazing lasagna. He always says, "I'm a Deluca. That's what you do on a holiday. You make lasagna."

"So, Jim, have you decided on a college yet?" Grandpa asked.

"Well, my applications are due next week," Jim replied. "And I've got a few in mind. But it will probably depend on which college will give me a football scholarship."

"Oh, that's wonderful, Jim!" Grandma said. "Just think, we might have a pro football player on our hands."

"The other night we were just talking about how we might have *two* pros in the family," Dad said proudly. "Jim in football and Elle in basketball."

I gave Jim a look that said *"Help!"* because I knew he hadn't decided whether or not to go pro for sure, either, and here was Dad pushing it again. But Jim was smiling at his girlfriend, Alyssa, and didn't notice me.

"Of course Elle will go pro!" Grandpa said. "Look how tall she is! She was born to play basketball."

There was that phrase again. *Born to play basketball*. Dad always said it, Blake had said it just the other day, and now Grandpa said it.

"That's right," Grandma said. "She's got the sporty gene from both sides of the family. I could have been a pro softball player, if there had been such a thing back then."

Uncle Danny nodded at me. "You're going to apply to UConn, right, Elle? They've got the best women's basketball team in the country."

"UConn, like University of Connecticut?" I asked.

Uncle Danny nodded. "All of the best WNBA players get their start there."

"Danny's right," Grandpa said. "You've got to aim for UConn, Elle. Start building your résumé."

"But I'm only in seventh grade," I said. "Isn't that a long way away?"

Blake's mom chimed in. "It's never too early to start. Blake is already looking at colleges."

I glanced at Blake and he shrugged. My head was spinning. Did I really have to think about colleges now? In seventh grade? And Connecticut was pretty far away. If I went there, I'd be far from Mom and Dad and Beth and Zobe. . . .

"Maybe I could go to a college in Delaware," I said meekly.

"You definitely need to look into UConn, Elle," Uncle Danny insisted. "You should aim for the top."

Aunt Jess smiled at me. "We'll be your biggest fans, Elle. We'll come to all your games, no matter where you end up playing."

Aunt Jess was talking like my future was already laid out, and that made me feel weird.

"Speaking of games, we're coming out for your game next Sunday, Elle," Grandma said.

Aunt Jess lit up. "Next Sunday? We should come too. The kids would love to see you play, Elle."

"The games are really exciting," Dad said. "And Elle is a star on the court."

"Wow, thanks, everybody," I said, and suddenly felt confused. It was nice to be good at something (most of the time) and to be praised for it by my family and friends. But what if I was also good at something else, something I didn't even know I was good at yet? Like . . . building robots, or sculpting, or cooking? I would never know if I spent all my time playing basketball.

And yet when dinner was over and Jim called for a game outside in the driveway, I was on my feet and out the door, eager to play.

We formed two teams: Me, Blake, and Uncle Danny against Dad, Jim, and Alyssa, who plays basketball on the Spring Meadow High School team. I didn't really know her that well, since Jim had just started dating her, but she seemed nice. She'd even brought basketball shoes with her since Jim told her we always play on Thanksgiving.

We flipped a coin, and Dad's team got the ball first.

"Man-to-man—I mean, player-to-player defense!" Uncle Danny called out. "Blake, you're on Jim. Elle, you've got Alyssa. I've got your dad."

"Brother against brother!" Jim joked.

But my dad and Uncle Danny took the game

seriously, even though it was a half-court family game after a big meal.

"Since this is half-court, every shot is two points," Uncle Danny said. "Make it or take it. First team to thirty wins, but you have to win by two."

"Make it or take it?" Alyssa asked.

"The team that makes the shot gets control of the ball afterward," Uncle Danny said.

Alyssa looked a little surprised. "Oh, okay. That's not how I usually play pickup."

"It's the Deluca way," Jim told her. "Family pickup rules."

"Let's get this game going!" Dad yelled, clapping his hands together, and Jim tossed him the ball.

For Dad's first move, he dribbled to the basket, and Uncle Danny was on him like glue. When Dad faked left and then tried to take a shot, Uncle Danny anticipated him and slapped the ball away. It bounced a few times, and in the skirmish I caught it, then jumped up and tossed the ball over Alyssa's head toward the basket. It slipped through with a satisfying swish.

"You've got to stay on top of Elle, Alyssa," Jim said. "She's a powerhouse."

"Yeah, and she's got four inches on me," Alyssa said with a grin.

Uncle Danny high-fived me. "Keep playing like that, Elle, and we'll take this!"

But right after my basket, Jim took the ball from Blake and scored two points. Then Uncle Danny scored. Then my dad. Then me again. Then Alyssa. The back-and-forth kept going until both teams were tied: 28–28.

Uncle Danny was in the right corner of the court closest to the basket, and he had control of the ball. Dad was right in his face and Uncle Danny could not make a move. I ran to the left side of the court.

"Sideways!" I called out, and Uncle Danny turned toward me and passed me the ball. Dad reached for it but he couldn't get it. Alyssa was on me, but Uncle Danny passed it super high. I jumped up and caught it. And right after my feet hit the ground, I made the shot.

Swish!

"Team Danny wins!" my uncle cried.

I looked at Blake and laughed. "I didn't know we were Team Danny."

"How about a rematch?" Jim asked.

Blake shook his head. "I don't think I can. It's almost five, right?"

My dad looked at his watch. "Yup."

"Yeah, well, I have to go," Blake said, and I could swear he was blushing.

"Go where?" I asked him suspiciously.

"Well, um, Bianca asked me over to watch the game this afternoon, and so . . ."

My eyes got wide. "You're hanging out with Bianca? But we always watch the game here."

"Yeah but, you know," Blake replied.

"No, I *don't* know," I said, and I could hear a tightness in my voice.

"It's no big deal," Blake said. "I'd invite you, but you and Bianca aren't exactly friends."

"No, we're not," I said. "Which is why I don't

get why you're ditching me to hang with her."

Blake sighed. "I'm not ditching you! We can hang out this weekend."

"Whatever," I said, and I turned away from him.

"I gotta go let my mom know that I'm leaving," Blake said. "Bye, everybody!" And he ran inside the house.

"We can play HORSE," Alyssa suggested.

"Yeah, sure," I said, even though I knew it wouldn't be as fun without Blake. And plus, I was having kind of dark thoughts about Bianca.

She was ruining basketball for me. Was she going to ruin my friendship with Blake too?

Blake's Secret

Friday morning I slept later than usual. Zobe did, too, because he was so tired from being chased by my little cousins yesterday after we'd let him out of the basement.

What woke me up was a beeping sound from my phone. A message in purple letters from the U-Plan app appeared on my screen.

Did you forget to walk Zobe, Elle?

"No," I said aloud. "I'm going to walk him."

Then I realized I was talking to my phone and felt a little silly.

"Come on, Zobe," I said, stretching. "Time to wake up and . . . do stuff."

My aunt and uncle and cousins had left the night before, but Grandma and Grandpa had slept over. When I got into the kitchen after letting Zobe out back, Grandma was placing a big platter of potato pancakes on the table.

"I made them with the leftover mashed potatoes," she said. "The fridge is so full of leftovers I had to do something!"

"They look great, Grandma," I said as I took a seat. Beth was at the table, too, and Mom was helping her with breakfast.

"You gotta put the applesauce on them," Grandpa said. "That's the best way."

"Sure," I said.

My phone flashed again with another message from U-Plan.

Zobe needs a walk, Elle!

"I'll do it as soon as I eat!" I snapped, and when I looked up, Mom, Grandma, and Grandpa were staring at me.

"It's my scheduling app," I said. "I like it, but the notifications are a little annoying."

"What's on your schedule for tomorrow?" Mom asked. "We're planning to get a Christmas tree."

I looked at my phone. "I have free time in the morning and study time in the afternoon," I said. Then I looked at my day today. "Hey, can Avery come over this afternoon? She's dying to meet Zobe."

"Oh, we'll have to stay and see Avery!" Grandma said. "She's such a sweet girl."

"That's fine with me," Mom said.

I texted Avery.

C u at 2! Zobe can't wait!

☺ she texted back.

"Avery, just look at you! You're so grown-up!" my grandmother said when Avery came over that afternoon.

"Nice to see you, Grandma," Avery said. (My grandmother likes all my close friends to call her "Grandma.")

Then Zobe came bounding to the front door.

"Zobe!" Avery cried as he put his two paws onto her shoulders. "Oh my goodness, you're beautiful! Look at that fur. It's gray, but it's almost got a bluish hue to it."

"They're called Blue Danes when they're this color," I told her.

"Can we take her for a walk?" Avery asked.

"Absolutely," I said. "He needs lots of exercise."

I hooked Zobe's leash to his collar and we brought him outside. Avery and I waited for him as he sniffed the lawn for a bit.

"I need to talk to you about those app notifications," I said. "I mean, I do love the app. This morning I caught up with all the reading I need to do for English. And you're finally meeting Zobe. But those notifications are a little annoying."

Avery smiled. "Yeah, sorry. You can turn them off. I left them on for you because I thought you might need them until you got used to the app."

"Thanks," I said. "You can show me when we get back."

Zobe started pulling on the leash, so we walked

down the driveway to the sidewalk and past Blake's house.

"Is Blake around?" Avery asked.

I shrugged. "I don't know," I said. "Yesterday he left Thanksgiving early to watch the game with Bianca."

Avery was silent, which I wasn't expecting. She should have responded with shocked disbelief . . . unless . . .

"What?" I asked. "Do you know something?"

Avery frowned. "Well, maybe I do," she said. "It's just—people are saying they're, like, a couple."

"A *couple*?" I asked. "Like dating?"

Avery nodded. "I know. It's weird, right?"

"Why didn't he tell me?" I asked. "I'm his best friend! He could have told me yesterday."

"I think it's because you really don't like Bianca," she replied.

"That's not true!" I protested. "I mean, I guess I don't like her much right now because she's giving me such a hard time. But I liked her before that. *She's* the one who started it!"

Avery looked thoughtful. "Hmm. Do you think she's jealous of your friendship with Blake?"

"That would be dumb," I said. "Blake and I are just normal friends."

"You don't *like* like him?" Avery asked.

"You know I don't!" I shuddered. "Ew! That would be weird. I don't like any boys like that."

Avery nodded. "Yeah, I know. It's just a lot of people assume you and Blake like each other because you do a lot of stuff together."

"That is *really* dumb," I said. "Why can't boys and girls be friends? Is there some kind of rule or something?"

"I don't know," Avery said.

We walked without talking for a few minutes as Zobe led us around the neighborhood.

"He should have told me," I said finally.

"Well, you can always tell him that you know," Avery suggested. "Talk to him. I mean, you're not mad that he's dating Bianca, are you?"

"No," I said. "I mean, I don't know. Bianca's being pretty terrible to me these days. If Blake were a real friend, he wouldn't hang out with her. But it's complicated, I guess."

"Definitely," Avery agreed.

We were quiet for another minute, and then I asked, "Do you *like* like anybody?"

Avery shook her head. "No. Not like that," she said. "I mean, just because we're in seventh grade doesn't mean we have to, does it?"

"Definitely not," I said, relieved. Things might have been complicated with Blake, but I was glad that with Avery everything was staying just the same.

After our walk, Avery and I hung out for a while. We played a board game with my grandparents before they drove back to Philly. And before Avery left, she helped me turn off the notifications on my app. I was pretty confident that I would be able to check the app every day on my own.

On Saturday the whole family took the van out to Van Houten's Tree Farm to pick out a Christmas tree. Even though it's kind of a long trip, we always bring Beth, because the smell of the pine trees makes her happy.

I know not every family puts up a Christmas tree right after Thanksgiving weekend, but my Dad is Christmas crazy.

"I would put up the tree on Thanksgiving night if your mom would let me," he always says. But he settles for Saturday, when we drive out to the country to pick out a tree from the farm. The air is so clean and fresh out there that I can understand why it makes Beth happy.

After we got our tree, we brought it home. Like always, Dad put on some Christmas music and Mom made hot cocoa, even though it wasn't that cold (it almost never gets really cold in Delaware). Jim and I helped get the decorations out of the attic, and we put the lights and ornaments on the tree. Then Jim and I helped Dad hang lights outside, wrapping them around the big maple tree in the front yard and on the front railings.

After we finished the trees, Dad climbed up a ladder while I held it steady, and Jim handed him icicle lights to hang across the front of the house.

"I prefer colored lights," Dad said, like he does

every year, "but your mom insists on white lights. So we are a white-light house."

"It's still pretty," I replied, like I do every year. And then, when the icicles were up, we got the light-up reindeer family out of the garage. Their bodies are made of wire, and white lights are wrapped around them. There are five, representing one for each Deluca.

It was dark by the time we finished, which was perfect. I always love the moment when Dad plugs in the lights and everything brightens. This year was no different. Mom came out to watch and brought Beth with her.

"One, two, three!" Dad counted down, and then everything lit up.

"Woo!" Jim cheered.

The lights looked beautiful. I reached out and grabbed Beth's hand. It always makes me a little bit sad to know that she can't see them. But sometimes I think that she can feel them, somehow. That she can feel their glow and their warmth and their peacefulness.

After getting all my homework, decorating, and Zobe-walking done, I was pretty tired. The next day, Sunday, I woke up wondering what to do with my free time since I didn't have a game. Hang out with Avery again, or maybe Caroline? Get Mom to take me to the mall so I could look at basketball shoes?

Then it hit me—even though I was happy not to have a game, I still wanted to play. After breakfast I took the ball out to our driveway and practiced some of the new drills that Coach had taught us. And Jim played a couple of games of one-on-one with me.

Maybe I was born to play basketball after all, I thought. But that thought only confused me more. How could I really be sure?

The whole time I was outside I kept glancing over at Blake's house. On any other day he would have come over to play with me. But he didn't, and I kept thinking that he was probably with Bianca. And I still didn't understand why he would hang out with her.

"Jim, when do things stop getting so confusing?" I asked him as I recovered a ball that he'd just bounced off the backboard. I figured he would know. He seemed to have it all together—he was a football star, he got great grades, and he had a nice girlfriend.

"Honestly, Elle, I don't think it ever does," he replied.

That surprised me, but I didn't ask him why. I didn't think I wanted to know. Instead I dribbled up to the basket and sank a layup.

That, at least, wasn't confusing at all.

Bianca Calls Me Out

A dendrite receives impulses from other neu-
rons, and carries those impulses to the cell
body," my science teacher, Ms. Rashad, was
saying. "The axon is a part of a neuron that carries
messages away from the cell body."

It was Monday morning and I was realizing that
there were still things even more confusing than
Blake liking Bianca. Specifically, the human nervous
system.

We had just finished a unit on cells, and now
we were moving on to the nervous system. I'd had

trouble understanding all the cell stuff, and it was looking like learning about the nervous system was going to be just as challenging. And Ms. Rashad was giving us a quiz on Friday that was going to be 10 percent of our grade for the semester!

Then I remembered Tiff's promise that she would help me with science. Right then I decided I needed to take her up on it. I didn't know Tiff all that well— we mostly knew each other from playing on the Nighthawks—but she'd always been nice to me.

So that afternoon, I caught up to her as we walked across the field to the high school building. I lucked out because she wasn't walking with Bianca like she usually does.

"Hey, Tiff," I said. "Thanks for offering to help me study for science. Do you think we could do it before the quiz?"

"Sure, Elle," she replied. "When do you want to meet up?"

"Um, maybe Thursday after school?" I asked. I looked at my phone and saw I had study time blocked in. Perfect!

"Okay," Tiff said. "I live in Pine Brook, so you can ride to my house with me. And then maybe you could get a ride home?"

I nodded. "That shouldn't be a problem. I'll ask my mom," I said. *And I'll have to ask her to walk Zobe too,* I thought.

Tiff grinned at me. "I think it will be fun. And hopefully the nervous system won't get on your *nerves* anymore."

She smiled at me. I knew Tiff was really smart and a great basketball player, and even sewed her own hijabs to match her clothes and her school uniform. But I had never thought of her as funny before now.

I smiled back. "Great! Thursday."

A few minutes later we were out on the court, and with no game to review, we warmed up and started on drills.

"Wednesday was a lot of fun, but now it's time to get back to work," Coach announced. "I need you to form two lines."

We obeyed, and then she demonstrated the drill.

She dribbled both balls down the court, alternating between dribbling first with her left hand, and then her right hand. On the way back, she dribbled both balls at the same time. And she did it very, very fast.

"This will help with your ball-handling skills," she said. "I need each team to take two balls and take turns going up and down the court."

Dina and Patrice were at the head of both lines, and they made their way down the court. The balls got away from both of them after a few feet. Dina laughed, shook her head, and chased after her stray ball. But Patrice wasn't smiling at all. She looked nervous.

"This is about control, girls!" Coach yelled. "Focus on what your hands are doing."

A few more players took their turns, and each one of them lost control of the ball at least once— even Bianca! So I was determined to stay focused when it was my turn.

And I was. I dribbled both balls carefully up and down the court, focusing on my hands like coach said. And I kept up a pretty good pace, too.

When I returned to the line and handed the balls to Avery, I was expecting some praise from Coach. But do you know what she said? "Elle, you need to work on your form when you're dribbling," Coach said. "Keep those knees bent!"

"Yes, Coach!" I replied, but inside I was fuming. Hadn't she'd noticed I was the only one on the team who hadn't lost control of the ball?

Then we did a one-on-one defensive drill, where two players started at the free throw line. One player tossed the ball to the other player, and the offensive player had to try to get to a designated shooting area with no more than three dribbles and take a shot.

I thought it was going to be fun—until Coach paired me up with *Bianca*.

"Bianca, you're on defense," she said.

Bianca nodded to her, and we jogged to the line. Bianca tossed me the ball, her dark eyes focused right on mine. I pivoted to turn my back to her and started to dribble. One . . . two . . . three . . .

Bianca was right on me, but I used my height to my advantage. I jumped up to take my shot and she couldn't reach the ball. It bounced off the back-board into the net.

"Okay, now switch," Coach instructed.

The two of us got back on the line and I tossed the ball to Bianca. It should have been easy to block the shot because I'm so much taller than she is. But Bianca dribbled twice and pivoted quickly before she stopped. I tried to swat down the ball, but it wasn't within reach, and Bianca made her shot.

"Yes!" Bianca cheered. "Take that, Elle!"

I cringed. But did Coach call her out for bad sportsmanship? No.

"Nice, Bianca!" Coach said. "Elle, you can't rely on your height all the time. I need you to pay more attention to the offense, especially when you're doing one-on-one defense."

"Yes, Coach!" I said again.

And then Bianca did something I couldn't believe.

"Coach, doesn't this prove I should be center?" she asked in front of everybody.

My other teammates got quiet.

"Bianca, Elle, over here," she said with a nod of her head toward the sidelines. "Everybody else, keep up with the drill."

I could feel the eyes of the others watching Bianca and me as we walked to the side with Coach. I could feel my neck getting hot. Bianca had gone too far.

Coach took a deep breath—she looked a little flustered. But then she started talking, and her voice was sharp.

"Bianca, I need you to stop asking me to make you center," she said. "I am the coach, and it's my job to do what's best for the team."

"Yes, Coach," Bianca said, nodding.

To my own surprise, I blurted out, "Listen, Coach, if Bianca wants to be center, I don't mind. I liked being a shooting guard better anyway." I did like being shooting guard, and if it got Bianca off my back, I'd be a lot happier.

Coach shook her head. "See, I think we've found the problem with you, Elle. Your heart hasn't been in it. But now I need you to listen to me. Your height and your ball-handling skills could make you the best center in the league. Maybe the state. So I need you to stick with it. And give it your all."

Then she looked at Bianca. "And I need you to lay off Elle. That's my job. You are still my backup center, Bianca, and that's not going to change unless *I* decide it needs to change. Got it?"

"Yes, Coach," Bianca replied, and her voice sounded tight to me. I knew she wasn't happy.

"And what about you, Deluca? Are you in?" Coach asked.

"I'm in," I answered. I wasn't sure if I meant it, but at that moment, with Coach staring at me, I couldn't have answered with anything else.

"Good," Coach said. "Now both of you, get back on that court."

Bianca and I jogged back, avoiding each other's eyes. My answer to Coach Ramirez kept repeating in my brain.

I'm in.

That was a big promise on my part. But since I'd said it out loud, I knew that I would have to keep that promise.

I would have to become the best center I could be. And I knew I'd have to work extra hard to make that happen.

Amanda O'Connor

You're volunteering at Camp Cooperation at 3:00 p.m., Elle!

"I thought I turned those notifications off?" I muttered as I made my way to the elementary school building. They had stopped for a couple of days, and then suddenly started up again.

I loved volunteering at Camp Cooperation, so I didn't actually mind the reminder, but the way it flashed on and off on my phone screen was kind of annoying.

"Do you always talk to your phone?" a voice behind me asked in a friendly way.

I turned to see Amanda there, grinning.

"Hey," I said. "No, my phone was just telling me to go volunteer at Camp Cooperation. Which is what I am already doing."

"Me too!" Amanda said. "I'm glad Avery came up with the idea for the team to take turns getting on the schedule. I had fun the first time we did it."

We'd reached the multipurpose room and stepped inside. A few kids were running around, and others were sitting quietly at one of the round tables. Brian, one of the guys who runs the programs, called out to us when he walked in.

"Hi, Elle!" he said. "Hi, Amanda!"

"Elle's here!" An eight-year-old boy with blond hair ran up to us—Pete, Caroline's little brother. Pete is in the program because he's got Down syndrome. He's got a lot of energy and loves sports.

"Elle, Elle, can we play ball?" Pete asked.

"Wow, you've got a fan," Amanda said.

"Elle is the best!" Pete said. "She's the best at

everything! She's the best at basketball!"

"Pete is Caroline's little brother," I explained to Amanda. "You've probably seen him at our games."

Brian interrupted us. "I was just about to take some of the kids outside. Do you girls want to join us? Elle, I know that's where you like to be."

"Sure," Amanda and I both said at the same time, and we smiled at each other.

"Zap!" Amanda said, poking my arm.

"Zap?" I asked.

Amanda blushed. "Oh, sorry, it's a reflex. It's a game we play in my family, when two people say the same thing at the same time. Whoever gets zapped first can't talk until the other person says their name."

"So I can't talk?" I asked.

"Well, since you didn't know the rules, *that* wouldn't be fair, Elle Deluca," she said. Then she wiggled her eyebrows. "But next time, watch out!"

We headed outside with Brian and a few of the kids, while Janette and Vicky, the other two adults who ran the program, stayed inside with the rest. The kids who liked to be outdoors were usually the same: Pete, Addie, Lily, and Max, who is Pete's friend. He has autism, like some of the other kids in the program. He didn't always join in when we played sports, but he liked to watch everybody play.

"What should we play today?" I asked the kids.

"Kickball! Kickball! Kickball!" Lily yelled.

Lily has autism like Max, but she is very loud and energetic. I knew that playing a game with just me, Amanda, Pete, Addie, and Lily might not work so well, so I had another idea.

"Let's have kicking practice," I suggested. "Lily, please go get the orange ball from the pile."

She ran to get it. I turned to Amanda. "Maybe we can do something with the cones?"

Amanda's green eyes lit up. "Yeah, that would be cool."

Amanda got five cones from the side of the elementary school field and set them up in a rough circle.

"Everybody stand in front of a cone," she said. "We can take turns kicking the ball to each other.

Then when everybody has had a turn, we'll all move to a different cone."

It was a simple game, and the kids got the hang of it pretty quickly. Everybody laughed when Pete kicked the ball so hard that it soared over Addie's head. She just stood there, giggling, and I yelled over to Brian and Max to ask them to help me fetch it. Brian picked up the ball and tossed it to me.

"We're going in for a snack in about five minutes," he told me.

"Okay," I replied. I couldn't believe how fast time went when I was playing with Pete and the other kids in the program. It made me a little bit sad that I was only coming two days a month now, even though it was better for my schedule.

We kicked the ball around some more, and when it was time for a snack, Pete started talking about basketball again.

"Elle, you're the best basketball player!" he said.

"You know, Amanda's on the team, too," I told him with a nod to her.

"I know. Amanda with the red hair," he said. "But you're the *best* player, Elle!"

I blushed a little, but Amanda laughed. "He's right, Elle."

"I don't know about that," I replied. "I didn't even score in the last game, Pete."

"It doesn't matter," Pete said. "You're still the best, Elle. I'm going to cheer for you on Sunday."

"Thanks, Pete," I said, but inside I could feel my stomach tightening a bit.

Grandpa and Grandma were also coming to the game to cheer for me. . . . What if I choked again?

Amanda must have been a mind reader or something, because while I was thinking this, she put her hand on my arm.

"Don't worry, Elle," she said. "You're going to do great on Sunday."

"Thanks," I replied. I just hoped she was right!

After the snack we went back outside and played for another half hour until it was time for the program to end. We said good-bye to Brian and the kids and then walked over to the high school entrance, the main pickup area at Spring Meadow.

"You know, we only live a few blocks away from each other," Amanda said. "You could always get a ride home with me if you need to sometime."

"Thanks," I said. "A lot of times I get a ride with Blake's mom, but . . ."

I didn't finish my thought, because that's when Mom pulled up to take me home. I waved to Amanda.

"See you tomorrow!" I said.

"For sure!" she replied with a grin.

"Amanda seems very nice," Mom remarked.

"She is," I said. "And she lives pretty close to us, by the park. She said on some days I could get a ride home with her if I ever need to."

"That would be very helpful," Mom said. "You know, I should reach out to her mom. What's her last name? I can find them in the school directory."

"O'Connor," I replied.

Amanda O'Connor, I repeated in my mind. And then, for some reason, I repeated it over and over on the ride home.

Amanda O'Connor. Amanda O'Connor. Amanda O'Connor.

When we pulled into the driveway I saw Blake sitting on his front steps, texting on his phone.

"I'll be inside in a minute," I told Mom, and she nodded and went inside the house.

I walked over to Blake.

"Hey, Elle!" he said.

"So you're, like, dating Bianca?" I blurted out.

Blake blushed. "Not dating, exactly. We hang out."

"So you *like* like her?" I pressed him.

"I think so," he said. "It's not a big deal. But I guess, technically, you could say she's my girlfriend."

"That's what Avery told me," I said, "which surprised me, because I figured you would tell me, your best friend, first."

"How could I tell you?" Blake argued. "You don't like Bianca."

"That's what you don't understand," I shot back. "I never disliked Bianca. It's only this year that she started dogging me about not being good enough to play center. She called me out in front of everyone on Monday. She's not being cool, Blake."

Blake shrugged. "She's competitive," he said. "What do you think the pros go through? People criticize them all the time. You have to be tough to play sports. Maybe you need to toughen up."

I was speechless for a second. Stunned, even. Blake and I had never had an argument in our whole friendship, but this was starting to feel like a fight.

"Whatever," I said quietly. "Do what you want."

And then I turned and walked back to my house. I took Zobe into the backyard and watched him run around.

I replayed the conversation (or was it a fight?) with Blake over in my mind. I had said that I had always liked Bianca, which was only partly true. Bianca and I had never really been friends. Sometimes she could be mean—like when she made fun of Brent McIntosh in gym for not being able to do a pull-up—and I just didn't like that about her.

But since Coach had moved me to center,

Bianca's mean comments had begun being directed at me. That's where the problem started. Blake had said that I should toughen up. Was that really the answer? Was I the problem and not Bianca?

I wasn't sure. But maybe Blake had a point. Maybe basketball would be easier for me if I grew a thicker skin.

Zobe ran up to me while I was thinking. I knelt down to scratch him behind the ears.

"What do you think, Zobe? Am I too fragile for basketball?"

In response, he licked my face, and I laughed.

Maybe I had to be tough to play basketball. But at home, I could just be myself—and that was nice.

The Coach's Daughter

This will be our last week of volleyball," Mr. Patel, our gym teacher, announced the next day.

A few kids cheered, and some of them groaned—including me. I really liked playing volleyball in gym class. I was pretty good at it and I thought it was fun.

"Those of you who like volleyball should consider joining the team," Mr. Patel went on. "This season is already underway, but you can play in the spring season."

I liked the idea of joining the volleyball team—

and then I remembered that the basketball travel team played in the spring. I'd joined the travel team for the first time last year, and the coaches all encouraged me to do it again this year. My coach had said that it was important to keep playing if you were serious about the sport. That meant summer basketball camp, too, which I had attended for the entire month of July, followed by a one-week intensive in August at the community college.

Mr. Patel divided us into teams, and I ended up on one with Hannah, Natalie, Blake, Dylan, and Jacob. When gym was over, after our team had won three straight games, Mr. Patel stopped me on the way to the locker room.

"You should really consider joining the volleyball team, Elle," he said. "They could use you."

"I'd like that a lot," I replied. "But you know—basketball."

"I understand," Mr. Patel said. "Do what makes you happy, Elle! Follow your bliss!"

Right after gym, I headed to lunch. Spring Meadow is a small school, and most of us have known one another since kindergarten. Since I started playing basketball in the third grade, I have sat at lunch with the same five girls: Avery, Natalie, Hannah, Caroline, and Patrice.

Avery, of course, is my best friend. Natalie and Hannah are best friends with each other. Natalie wears glasses, and over the summer she'd dyed a streak of her hair bright pink. While Natalie is outgoing, Hannah is more of an introvert. Hannah's dad, Mr. Chambal, is the one who records our games that Coach Ramirez plays back to us on Mondays.

Then there's Caroline. Even though I've known her for years, I didn't really know her that well. Her best friend is someone from her town, and she doesn't do a lot of school activities except for basketball. I only recently learned that it's because she spends a lot of time helping to take care of her brother Pete and her other brother, Sam.

Finally there's Patrice. She kind of looks like a mini version of her mom, Coach Ramirez, except Patrice wears her black hair long and pulls it into a ponytail. She's always been quiet and shy, so I don't know that much about her. I couldn't tell you who her best friend is, or even if she has a best friend at all.

What I knew about Patrice I mostly knew from the court. I knew that she worked really hard and she always did her best, even though she wasn't our best player. And her mom put her in to play a lot and was harder on her than almost anyone on the team—except maybe for me.

At lunch on Wednesday we started talking about the upcoming game on Sunday.

"So Sunday we're playing the Bobcats," Natalie announced, and then she gave a shudder.

All five of us groaned. The Bobcats are the team from Becker Heights Academy, another private school in Wilmington. Becker Heights and Spring Meadow have been rivals for a long time. And whenever the teams play each other, it can get ugly.

"I can't believe their coach lets them taunt us," Hannah said. "It's not very sportsmanlike."

"You mean sports*girl*like," Natalie corrected her.

"Is that a word?" Avery asked.

"It should be," Natalie replied. "We are not sports *men*!"

"Well, anyway, Hannah is right," Caroline said. "Their coach shouldn't let them do it, and the ref never stops it."

"They do it before the game starts, so they can't be penalized," Avery said.

I frowned. "Well, I don't see why they have to be mean just because we're rivals. We're not like that."

Then Patrice joined the conversation in a quiet voice. "Mom always gets really stressed when we play the Bobcats."

"I can imagine," Caroline told her. "That's gotta be stressful for you too, right?"

Patrice didn't answer. She just took a sip from her milk carton.

"I bet she's gonna work us extra hard at practice today," Natalie remarked, and then the rest of us got quiet, too, thinking about it.

A few hours later we realized how right we all were. Coach had us moving the second we came out of the locker room. We did squats, push-ups, and sit-ups. We ran around the gym twenty times. We did ball-handling drills, shooting drills, offensive drills, and defensive drills. And the word of the day was "focus."

"Focus on the ball!"

"Focus on your stance!"

"Focus on your opponent!"

It was an intense practice and we didn't joke around like we usually do. I felt relieved when it came time to scrimmage because I knew practice would be over soon.

The teams this time were me, Bianca, Caroline, Dina, and Patrice against Tiff, Avery, Natalie, Hannah, and Amanda. Coach had Tiff play center for her team, and she and I faced off at the start of the scrimmage. I tipped the ball and Bianca caught it. Patrice was open, so Bianca passed it to her.

The ball slipped right through Patrice's hands and bounced, and Amanda grabbed it away.

"Patrice, focus!" Coach yelled.

Dina managed to steal the ball from Amanda and took it down the court. She attempted a shot from the three-point range, but it bounced off the headboard. Luckily I was on top of it. I caught the rebound and sank an easy two-pointer.

"Good job, Elle!" Coach said. It was the first compliment she'd given me in a long time.

I made another basket a few minutes later, and my confidence started to build back up. Things weren't going so well for Patrice, though. She missed a layup, and Hannah got the ball away from her twice. Her mom called her out every time she made a mistake.

"More effort, Patrice!"

"Pivot, Patrice!"

"Don't let her dominate you, Patrice!"

I felt so bad for her. I mean, Coach was being harder than usual on Patrice. I tried to imagine my own mom barking criticism at me like that, and it made me feel bad just thinking about it.

Then right before the end of the scrimmage, Patrice ran out of bounds, trying to catch a pass from Dina.

"Patrice, that is a rookie move!" Coach yelled.

Patrice's face turned bright red. Then she burst into tears.

We all stopped playing except for Bianca, who had picked up the ball and was taking a shot at the basket.

"Yes!" she cried when the ball went in, oblivious to what was happening.

Sobbing, Patrice ran out of the gym.

All eyes turned to Coach Ramirez. She looked surprised but not angry.

"Practice is over," she said, in a voice about half as loud as normal. We all hesitated for a moment and then slowly headed to the locker room.

"Maybe we should go after Patrice," Hannah said in a loud whisper.

Avery looked behind us. "I think that's Coach's job. Poor Patrice."

I felt bad for Patrice, but I totally understood her. Sometimes I felt like running away when Coach Ramirez got on my case. Seeing Patrice do it made me wonder—would I be the next one to do that?

No, you will not, Elle! I told myself. *You are the new, tough Elle, remember?*

Everyone was still talking as we entered the locker room.

"I think the pressure got to her," Caroline remarked.

"I think it must be very hard to be the daughter of the coach," Tiff said thoughtfully.

Avery nodded. "Maybe Coach doesn't want anyone to think she's playing favorites with Patrice."

Dina snorted at that. "Then why does she always start her?"

"Well, I still feel sorry for her," Amanda said.

"Me too," I agreed. "I think her mom is really stressing her out."

Bianca rolled her eyes. "She needs to toughen up," she said, reminding me of Blake's defense of her the day before.

"That's kind of harsh," Natalie remarked.

Bianca shrugged. "Coaches are supposed to be tough. I don't think she's being too hard on Patrice. She's just being harder on the weakest players." She looked right at me when she said that.

"Do you mean me?" I asked her.

Bianca shrugged. "I'm just saying . . ."

"Well, Patrice isn't weak," I said. "She works hard

and she's a strong player. I don't blame her for running out like that."

"Well, of course you wouldn't," Bianca replied.

I was done dealing with Bianca. I couldn't even have a conversation with her anymore without her insulting me, and I didn't need that in my life.

I picked up my duffel bag and nodded to Avery. "Coming?"

Avery nodded and followed me.

"Whoa, that was intense," she said as we walked down the hallway. "Poor Patrice. And then Bianca called you out like that. She's unbelievable!"

I nodded. "I'm sick of it," I admitted. "And I stand by what I said about Patrice. She's under a lot of pressure."

I was under a lot of pressure too—from Coach and from Bianca, who was still hassling me even though Coach had asked her not to.

Could I keep dealing with the pressure—or would I crack, like Patrice had?

Brains and Tea

Lunch the next day began really awkwardly. Everyone wanted to talk to Patrice about what had happened, but nobody wanted to start the conversation. So nobody said anything.

After about five minutes of silence, Natalie couldn't take it anymore.

"So, Patrice, like, are you still on the team?" she asked.

At first Patrice looked a little bit like a deer in headlights. It didn't look like she was going to answer.

"Yeah, I'm still on the team," she said. "I . . . I'm sorry about yesterday. That was dumb."

That's when it hit me—none of us on the team were really that close to Patrice, and she didn't hang out with any of us outside of school. Was that because she was the coach's daughter? Maybe one of the reasons she had broken down the day before was because she didn't have anybody on the team she could really talk to about how her mom was treating her. We all had someone, except her.

"It wasn't dumb," I assured her. "Everybody understands. Don't sweat it."

"I'm glad you didn't quit," Natalie said. "We'd miss you!"

Patrice smiled a little. "Thanks. But you know, you'd still see me at lunch, even if I had quit."

Patrice's words got me thinking. I spent so much time with my basketball friends—at practice, at games, at after-game celebrations. I couldn't imagine only seeing my teammates at lunch or in class when we spend so much time together on the team. The thought of that changing was a little scary.

Then Hannah started talking about this podcast she listened to, and Patrice looked relieved that the subject had changed. I was still thinking that maybe it would be nice to get to know Patrice better, just in case she ended up quitting the team.

I quickly looked at my phone and realized that I had a study session with Tiff at her house after school. Had I told my mom? I sent her a quick text just in case.

After our last class, I waited in the front hall for Tiff.

"Thanks again for doing this," I said.

"No problem," Tiff said with a smile. "Come on, my mom is outside."

As we headed outside, it occurred to me that I was about to spend the afternoon with Bianca's best friend. Did Tiff feel the same way about me as Bianca did? Tiff had always been nice to me, but part of me couldn't help wondering.

We walked over to her mom's car, where Mrs. Kalifeh gave me a big smile. She had the same big, brown eyes as Tiff, and she wore a hijab that matched her blue dress.

"Hello, Mrs. Kalifeh," I said. "Thanks for the ride."

"No problem," she said.

I climbed into the back seat, where a boy who looked to be about Pete's age was sitting.

"Hello," he said politely. "I'm Jack."

"Hi, Jack," I said as I clipped in to my seat belt. "I'm Elle. Your sister's going to tutor me in science today."

"I think that Tiff would make a wonderful teacher," her mom said, "but she wants to be a doctor, you know."

"Wow, really?" I asked.

Tiff nodded and turned to the back seat to talk to me. "Yes, I think I want to study childhood diseases. Maybe work in a children's hospital."

"My sister, Beth, spent a lot of time in children's hospitals when she was growing up," I found myself saying. "Mom says the doctors there saved her life."

"Oh, your poor sister," Mrs. Kalifeh said. "How is she now?"

"Well, she's my older sister," I explained, and

then I told them about Beth, and how she'd had a bunch of surgeries when she was little, before I could remember. Tiff and her mom listened sympathetically.

"I'd love to be able to help kids like that someday," Tiff said.

"So you're not thinking of a career in basketball?" I asked.

Tiff shook her head. "No way. I do it because it's fun. And good exercise."

"And because she is very good at it," her mom added, and Tiff beamed with pride. "And you are too, Elle. Such a good player, and so tall. Perhaps you were destined to become a basketball player!"

There it was again—another person mentioning my height and basketball in the same sentence. I was starting to understand that I was probably going to hear people say stuff like this for the rest of my life.

Pretty soon we got to Tiff's home, a two-story brick house on a pretty, tree-lined street. Mrs. Kalifeh, Tiff, and Jack took their shoes off in the doorway, so I did, too, although I wished I had worn matching socks.

"Where are you going to study, Tiff?" her mom asked.

"I was thinking in my room," she said, and Mrs. Kalifeh nodded.

"Come down if you would like a snack," she said.

We walked upstairs to Tiff's room, and I marveled at how well organized it was. The walls were painted a cheerful pale yellow, and the bed was carefully made, with two flowery yellow throw pillows side by side on top. Her desk was neatly organized with a laptop and a metal pencil holder filled with pens and pencils. I didn't see any stray socks on the floor, like you might find in my room back home. I wondered if an organized mind is what you needed to be good at science.

Tiff took a white wooden chair from the corner and pulled it up to the desk, next to the desk chair. Then she sat down in the desk chair and motioned for me to sit next to her.

"I found some really fun science websites online,"

she said. "And they all have stuff about the nervous system.'"

She opened up her laptop. First she played a goofy kind of cartoon about the nervous system. It began with a cartoon guy wearing a funny hat, drinking a cup of steaming tea. When he put the tea to his mouth, his face turned red and steam came out of his ears.

"Aaaaaargh! My tea is too hot!" he cried.

Then a narrator came in and explained how the man's nervous system told him the tea was too hot. The animation changed to show a cartoon human brain, and the narrator started talking about the different parts of the brain.

"I'm glad this is just a cartoon brain," I whispered, and Tiff laughed.

It was a silly cartoon, but I had to admit that it helped me understand how the nervous system worked a little better. After that, Tiff showed me a site with a quiz that I could take. I didn't get all the answers right the first time, but when I took it again, I got a lot more right than on my first try.

"Wow, this is really helpful," I said. "Thanks."

"Do you have any questions?" she asked. "Anything that's really confusing?"

"I guess it's that whole thing about involuntary movements," I said. "They're just controlled by one part of the brain?"

"Right, the brain stem," she said. "Each part of the brain has a different function—just like the players on a team."

I nodded. "Okay." Somehow Tiff relating the brain to basketball got me to relax about the whole science thing. We did some online flash cards next, and I pretty much aced them.

"Tiff, you would definitely make a good teacher," I said.

She smiled. "Thanks. Want to eat something before your mom picks you up? I'm starving."

"Sure," I agreed.

We went downstairs, where Mrs. Kalifeh had put out a plate of cookies for us. Tiff walked over to a teapot on the stove and poured the tea into two tiny, cute teacups with an intricate black and gold pattern.

"I hope you like tea," she said. "We drink a lot of it in this house. It's pretty big in Egypt."

"I like it," I said. "I mean, I usually drink iced tea. I don't know if I've ever had hot tea before."

She put a spoonful of sugar into my cup and stirred it for me. "In that case, it should be a little sweet for your first time," she said.

We sat down at the kitchen table and picked up our cups. Then we both looked at each other, grinning.

"Ahhhh! My tea's too hot!" we both exclaimed, and then we burst into giggles.

Mrs. Kalifeh came into the kitchen. "Is everything all right?"

"Sorry, Mom," Tiff replied. "We were just goofing on this science video we saw."

Mrs. Kalifeh shook her head and left the room.

"Seriously, though, the tea is pretty hot," Tiff said. She blew on her cup, and I did too. Then I took a sip.

"It's good," I said. "Thanks."

I picked up a cookie. "Yum, oatmeal. I love oatmeal," I said.

"Chocolate chip is my favorite," Tiff said. "But I like oatmeal, too."

"Oh, then you would love these oatmeal–chocolate chip cookies that my mom and I make," I said. "They combine the best of two awesome cookies to make the ultimate cookie."

Tiff nodded. "That sounds really good," she said, and I made a mental note to bake some for her to thank her for helping me study.

Then she took a sip of her tea. "So, um, you know I'm friends with Bianca, right?" she asked.

I nodded. "Yeah," I said. "I was worried it might be weird with us hanging out since Bianca doesn't seem to like me very much."

"I don't think she doesn't like you," Tiff said. "It's just—she was really devastated when Coach said she couldn't play center. It upset her a lot. I know she's being kind of hard on you, but it's just because she wants everyone to play their best so the team can win."

"Yeah, well, I didn't ask to be center," I pointed out. "And by constantly riding me, she's stressing me out. So if she really wants me to play better, she should back off."

Tiff shrugged. "You know the part of the brain that controls rational behavior? Neuroscientists actually think they don't fully develop in humans until age twenty-five. My mom says that explains why kids make so many mistakes. She doesn't mean it in a bad way—she says we can't always help it. That it's part of learning how to be an adult."

"Wow," I said. "I think *my* brain is going to explode from all this brain stuff. But I think I get what you mean."

Tiff nodded. "Try not to take it personally. Bianca will come to her senses."

I took another sip of tea. "Thanks," I said.

Tiff had made me feel a little bit better about Bianca, but just a little. Anyway, I was done talking about Bianca. I wanted to get to know Tiff better.

"So, do you ever visit Egypt?" I asked. "I loved it when we did that unit on ancient Egypt last year. I like history a lot better than science."

"Sometimes we go visit in the summer," Tiff

replied. "I wasn't born there, like my parents were, so it's really exciting for me. For them, they mostly go to see family and their old friends."

My phone beeped with a text from Mom.

Okay if I pick you up in ten?

I texted her back with a thumbs-up emoji.

"My mom's coming soon," I said. "Thanks a lot. For everything."

"No problem," Tiff said. "And tomorrow I know you are going to slay that quiz!"

Zobe Makes a Friend

Which part of the brain controls balance, coordination, and movement?

I wrote down the answer confidently on my quiz: *the cerebellum.* Then I got distracted, wondering if my cerebellum was the reason I'd kept tripping over my feet ever since my big growth spurt. I had always blamed my feet, but should I have blamed my cerebellum?

Luckily I refocused on the test and kept answering more questions. After my study session with Tiff I felt totally confident. I was sure I had aced it!

I was still feeling confident when I got to practice that afternoon. Patrice was there, like she'd said she would be, but she didn't look happy to be there at all.

When we came into the gym, Coach was pacing back and forth.

"Sunday's an important game," she said right off the bat. "I don't have to tell you that Spring Meadow has a long-standing rivalry with the Bobcats. I've been watching some of their game footage online, and they look really good this year. Their offense in particular is really strong. So today we're going to do some more defensive drills."

She led us through another grueling practice, just as she had on Wednesday. Squats. Push-ups. Sit-ups. Jumping jacks. More squats. Then a bunch of fast-paced drills.

For the scrimmage, Coach put me and Bianca on opposite teams again. It was me, Avery, Caroline, Amanda, and Patrice against Bianca, Tiff, Dina, Hannah, and Natalie.

Bianca and I faced off again at the start of the

game. I looked her right in the eyes, determined not to let her get to me. I hit the ball to Avery and ran past Bianca. Avery passed it to me, and I took it down the court. I stopped in the two-point zone and made the shot.

"Yay, Elle!" Amanda called out.

I smiled and kept pushing through the scrimmage. For the first time, Coach kept mostly quiet as we played, and I wondered if it had something to do with Patrice's meltdown. But I pushed that thought aside and concentrated on playing the best game that I could.

Almost every time I got the ball, I got myself in a position to shoot—and I made every shot I took, except for one that went a little too far to the right. When the scrimmage ended, our team had beat Bianca's 24–19. My teammates and I high-fived one another.

"I saw a lot of good effort from most of you out there," Coach told us. "Everybody needs to give a hundred and ten percent on Sunday, though. See you in Becker Heights."

I was feeling pretty great. Coach hadn't been too hard on me, and Bianca hadn't made any comments about me, either. But on the way to the locker room, Coach stopped me.

"Elle, I need to see you for a sec," she said.

Avery shot me a curious look as she headed into the locker room without me.

To be honest, I was expecting Coach to compliment me on playing a good scrimmage. But that's not at all what she did.

"Elle, you scored a lot today," she said. "And that's good, but there were several times you could have passed to teammates who were in a better scoring position. Trying to score all the points yourself isn't always the best strategy. The Bobcats have a strong defense, too, so you might not to be able to get into a shooting position each time you get possession of the ball. You need to pay attention to what else is happening on the court."

I nodded. "Okay," I replied, but my stomach had tightened into a little ball.

Coach Ramirez hadn't said anything that wasn't

true. The problem was it wasn't what I'd wanted to hear. In that moment it felt like she was putting me down. Like always. No matter how hard I tried, or how well I played, she would still have only negative things to say.

I ran into the locker room and grabbed my duffel bag. The other girls had left, but Avery was waiting for me.

"What was that about?" she asked.

"I just can't win," I replied, getting more and more upset. "No matter how I play, Coach criticizes me. I could score a thousand points and she'd come down on my footwork after the game or say someone else should be taking the shots. It's not fair."

"Do you think maybe she's just hard on you because you're such a good player?" Avery asked. "It could be a coaching strategy."

"Or maybe I'm just not as good as she wants me to be," I said.

"Elle, you *are* good!" Avery said. "Stop doubting yourself."

"You mean toughen up?" I asked with a weak smile.

"No, just be more confident. Embrace your awesomeness," Avery said. Then she changed the subject. "So, how's Zobe doing?"

"Dad and I are taking him to his first obedience class tomorrow," I told her. "I'm a little nervous."

"Zobe's going to do great," Avery assured me. "He's a good boy."

"Bad boy, Zobe!" I scolded him.

It was Saturday morning and Dad and I had brought Zobe to Human Training for Dogs, a dog training center in a strip mall in Greenmont. As soon as we stepped into the large training room, Zobe had strained his leash to pounce on a tiny Chihuahua.

"I'm so sorry," I told the woman holding the Chihuahua's leash. She had short gray hair and glasses, and she looked a little frightened of Zobe.

"That's all right," she said. "I think Bruiser likes Zobe."

I looked down at the little dog, white with brown

ears and shiny black eyes. He was bravely sniffing one of Zobe's paws, even though it was as big as his own head.

"Bruiser's a great name," my dad said. "I'm Eddie, and this is my daughter Elle."

"Nice to meet you. I'm Betty," she said. "I've had Bruiser for a year now, but he causes me so much trouble sometimes. He barks at the slightest noise. And when I walk him in the park, he barks at every dog he sees! I'm very surprised he's not barking at Zobe."

I glanced at Zobe, who was sniffing Bruiser's butt. I sighed.

"Zobe!" I said.

"Zobe is a new addition to our household," Dad explained. "There's a lot he needs to learn."

"I want to train him to be a therapy dog one day," I added. "He's so sweet. I think he would be great at it."

Betty patted Zobe's head. "He does seem like a sweetheart," she said. "I was in the hospital a few years ago, and the visits from the therapy dog there really made me feel better. That's why I got Bruiser."

Now the little dog was whining, and Betty reached down and picked him up. "That's a good boy, Bruiser. Mommy loves you."

Zobe looked at me and whined.

"If you think I am picking you up, you are crazy," I said, and Betty laughed.

Then a woman walked into the room, leading a brown and white dog with fluffy fur and bright blue eyes. She wore her gray-streaked hair in a long side braid, and her blue T-shirt had the letters HTFD on it.

"Hey, everyone, can we please form a big circle?" she asked.

The chatter in the room stopped and everyone started to move. Besides Betty and Bruiser, I counted seven other dogs and their owners. I saw a Boston terrier, a poodle, and a furry brown mutt. There was a fluffy white dog, a dog with short, orangey fur, and a gray dog with bluish fur that reminded me of Zobe's, but this dog was not anywhere near as big and had a face almost like a wolf. There was also a dog that looked like a German shepherd, but even she didn't come close to being as big as Zobe.

"I'm Valerie, and this is Human Training for Dogs," she said. "Now, you might think that's a strange name for a dog training school. But here we believe that people need to be trained to work with their dogs—not the other way around. So this is just as much about you as it is about your pet. Now, let's go around the circle and introduce yourself and your dog."

Everybody took turns. It turned out that the gray dog was an Australian cattle dog named Edna that had been rescued from a shelter in Virginia.

"Australian cattle dogs are noted for being very smart," Valerie said, and she glanced down at her dog. "They are cousins to Australian shepherds, like Bruce here. Right, Bruce?"

Bruce barked.

Then Valerie looked at the poodle owner. "Poodles are very smart too."

She didn't say anything about Great Danes, and I felt bad for Zobe. I knew he was smart too!

"We're going to begin by learning some simple

commands," Valerie said. "We use a method called treat training."

She walked around the circle and handed every dog owner a pouch of tiny brown treats. I opened the bag and made a face. The treats smelled terrible!

"These are liver treats," Valerie said. "Dogs love them. For training, you only need a tiny piece of a treat. Keep it closed in your hand, like this." She demonstrated for us. Then she turned and faced her dog, Bruce.

"First we're going to learn the 'come' command," Valerie said. "Take your dog off the leash and walk backward a few feet. Now get in a squatting position, like this, and open your arms."

She demonstrated by getting into the position in front of her dog.

"Bruce, come!" Valerie said.

Bruce trotted right to Valerie, and she reached out and patted his head. "Good boy!"

Valerie stood up. "Call your dog in a positive, cheerful voice. If your dog comes toward you, praise him. When he gets close to you, don't reach out and try to grab him. That will startle him. When he gets close enough to pet, give him praise and then give him the treat."

I looked at Dad. "Should I do it?"

He nodded. "Sure. Then maybe I'll do the next one."

I unhooked Zobe's leash. Before I could even take one step backward, he darted over to Bruiser and started trying to play with him.

"Zobe!" I scolded, and I quickly put him on the leash and brought him back to Dad.

"That's okay," Valerie said. "Just keep him on the leash for now, Elle."

I nodded and tried it again with Zobe on the leash. He watched me as I walked back a few steps.

"Zobe, come!" I called.

But he only pulled on the leash, trying to get to Bruiser.

"Move slowly toward him, Elle," Valerie coached. "Lead him back to the spot where you want him to be. And praise him, don't scold him."

I took a deep breath.

"Good boy, Zobe, you can do it," I said. "Now we're going to try this again."

I walked backward a few steps. I squatted and opened my arms wide.

"Zobe, come! Come here!"

Zobe bounded toward me and knocked me right on my back!

"Well, at least he came," I said as I sat up. "Right?"

"Try it again, Elle," Valerie instructed. "Praise him when he gets close. Give him the treat before he can jump on you."

I couldn't help but notice that all the other dogs were doing great. I sighed. I knew that Zobe could do better. In my heart I knew that he was the best dog in the room!

Then it hit me. Was I expecting great things out of Zobe the way Coach was expecting great things out of me?

"Come, Zobe!" I said, and this time he trotted up to me.

"Nice and easy, Zobe!" I said. "Good boy!"

When he got close enough, I put my hand up to

his snout and let him eat the treat. He gobbled it up, and I patted his head.

"Good dog!" I said. "Good dog, Zobe!"

Then I had a silly thought.

Maybe if Coach gave me treats every time I did something right, I wouldn't mind so much when she gave me a hard time!

Down to the Wire

When obedience class was over, Zobe and Bruiser were still sniffing each other and playing.

"I don't think Bruiser wants to leave," Betty said. "These two seem to have become good friends very quickly."

I had an idea. "Do you live in Greenmont? Do you ever take Bruiser to the dog park?"

Betty nodded. "In the mornings, usually," she said.

"Well, maybe they can hang out there together

some time," I said. "I mean, I have school in the mornings. So maybe on the weekends, when I'm not playing basketball."

Betty smiled. "That would be lovely," she said. "And how nice that you play basketball. I played in high school, you know. But I'm too short for the sport, so I didn't get much time on the court. Oh my goodness! I just made a poem."

"It was nice meeting you, Betty," Dad said. "See you next week!"

As we drove home, I was thinking about a lot of things. About how cute Zobe and Bruiser were together. But also about Betty, and how she said she'd been too short to be good at basketball. I knew there had been some great short players in the WNBA—as short as five foot two and a half—but Betty looked even shorter than that.

What if I had been very, very short instead of very, very tall? One of the reasons I had started watching the WNBA was because I liked how most of the players were tall like I was. Would I still have become obsessed with the WNBA? Would I have played games in the driveway with Jim? Would I even have started playing basketball—and if I did, if I loved it, would I still have been good at it? I had always thought that being freakishly tall (my mom hates when I say that, but it feels true to me) was some kind of curse, but what if it was the only thing that had led me to basketball?

Then I thought about the flip side. That maybe if I had been short, I would have gotten interested in gymnastics, or photography, or something besides basketball. I might have turned out to be a completely different person. A completely different Elle. Maybe she did exist out there in an alternate universe. *Was short Elle happy?* I wondered. *Was Bianca still mean to short Elle, or were they good friends?*

"Penny for your thoughts, Elle?" Dad said, and I realized I was staring out the passenger window in a daze.

I tried to imagine explaining everything going on in my cerebrum (the part of the brain that controls thinking, which I knew thanks to Tiff), but that would be impossible. So I just said, "Thinking about the game against the Bobcats tomorrow."

Dad nodded. "Yeah, there's always extra pressure when the Nighthawks and the Bobcats face off. But don't worry, Elle. Just do your best, like you always do."

"I will," I promised.

I can't say I wasn't nervous when I woke up on Sunday morning. I was. Grandma and Grandpa were coming to the game, along with Uncle Danny, Aunt Jess, and my cousins. Pete was going to be rooting for me too. So the pressure was on for this game— especially since I'd failed spectacularly during my last game.

But even though I was nervous, I wasn't psyching myself out like I had done two weeks before. I think it was thanks to Avery reminding me to be confident. And Coach telling me I could be the best in the state if I gave it my all. And even Blake telling me to toughen up.

You are going to ace this game, Elle, I told myself, and I believed it.

I started my pregame ritual. I do the same thing before each game to bring me luck, just like most of the players in the WNBA. I walked and fed Zobe, did thirty minutes of shootout practice in the driveway, then showered, ate half a bagel with peanut butter, and took a nap.

When I got dressed, I put on my socks and shoes *before* I put on my shorts, right foot first, so I could start the game on the right foot. I know that all might sound weird, but two weeks ago was the first time in years that I couldn't do my routine (long story, but I had to study instead). I was convinced that was part of the reason I hadn't scored one shot last game and I didn't want to take any chances.

"It's chilly outside, Elle!" Mom called up the stairs. "Wear your hoodie!"

I grabbed my hoodie from the pile of clothes in the corner of my room (and thought briefly that Tiff would never put her clothes in a pile) and bounded downstairs. I was ready for this game. Ready to prove what I could do.

Mom and Dad drove me to Becker Heights

Academy for the game. Now, Spring Meadow is a really nice place to go to school. The three different school buildings look pretty much like regular old school buildings made of bricks. The grounds are beautiful, and there is an actual meadow with wildflowers that bloom in the spring.

However, Becker Heights Academy is *much* fancier. The main building looks almost like a large mansion, with a round tower on the top. As we drove up to the parking lot it gleamed bright white against the blue fall sky. Rows of maple trees with beautiful orange leaves lined the drive. The trees looked like they had changed color at the exact same moment. Everything about Becker Heights looked absolutely perfect.

We drove around to the rear parking lot in front of the gymnasium building, a long, one-story building also painted white. I could see that some of the Nighthawks had started to arrive—and then I spotted Grandma and Grandpa getting out of their car.

I climbed out of our car and ran over to hug them.

"Thanks for coming to the game!" I said.

"It's about time we came," Grandma replied.

"Knock 'em dead, Elle!" Grandpa said.

"I will, Grandpa!"

I ran inside the gym, took off my hoodie, and tossed it on the sidelines. Then I joined the other Nighthawks on the side of the court. Avery, Bianca, and Tiff were already stretching, and I joined in. I was starting to feel really pumped up for the game.

Then Coach Ramirez came in with Patrice.

"Stretch it out, girls," she instructed. "We're going to start our shooting drills in a minute."

"Yes, Coach!" we all answered, and I could hear the energy in everyone's voices.

Then we heard the voices of the Bobcats.

"How do you spell loser? N-I-G-H-T-H-A-W-K-S! Whooo!"

We all turned to see the Bobcats in their brown and white uniforms, standing in a circle as they delivered their taunting chant.

"Line up for the shooting drill!" Coach called out, ignoring the team's nasty cheer.

We quickly split up into two groups of five and lined up on the free throw lane lines for the drill. Even though I was doing my best to stay focused, I spotted Pete on the Nighthawks side of the fans, and also Blake, to my surprise. He usually didn't come to games. Was he there for me, or for Bianca, or both of us? Why did it matter to me?

Focus! I scolded myself, and pushed the thought outside my head. We had a team to beat.

After we'd been drilling for a few minutes, the ref blew his whistle.

At Coach's command, five of us ran out onto the court and took our positions: me, Bianca, Avery, Patrice, and Tiff, who wore her yellow and green hijab she'd made that matched our uniforms perfectly.

"Destroy them!" somebody yelled out from the Bobcats side of the stands.

I tuned it out. I faced the Bobcats center, who was about two inches shorter than I was. She glared at me with her icy blue eyes.

Then the ref tossed the ball, and I sprang up like

I had rockets in my shoes. I tipped the ball to Avery. She had three Bobcats surrounding her, but she pivoted and found a space to pass the ball to Bianca. Bianca tore down the court and made a layup.

"Yes!" I cheered. What a great start to the game!

One of the Bobcats threw the ball in, and number 27 caught it—a girl with her light brown hair in a long braid. She took it down the court, but Tiff was on her. Number 27 dribbled around the perimeter of the three-point line, trying to find a way in or a free player to pass to. Finally she decided to pass, and Tiff slapped it in midair. Tiff couldn't recover it, but Bianca swooped in and got it for our team.

She dribbled it down to the three-point line and passed it to Patrice, who was open. Patrice took a shot and missed, and one of the Bobcats grabbed the rebound. We chased the Bobcats back down the court as they passed it back and forth to each other. Number 27 got it right in front of the basket, but Tiff jumped up and blocked the shot, grabbing the ball.

Tiff dribbled away and passed it to me. I dribbled,

taking three big strides toward the three-point line and stopped. Nobody was on me, so I took the shot.

Swish! Nighthawks were off to a good start, with a score of 5–0.

The Bobcats fought back, though. One of them dribbled the ball down the court and passed it to 27. She managed to take a shot this time, but it fell short of the basket. Her teammate caught the rebound, passed it to another Bobcat, and this time, the shot was good.

Immediately the fans in the stands started to sing. "Na-na-na-na, hey, hey, hey, good-bye, Nighthawks!"

Besides being annoying, it was also kind of a silly thing to chant when your team was still three points behind. But I tried to tune it out. The Nighthawks had control of the ball, and Avery dribbled the ball down the court, guarded by one of the Bobcats. She managed to pass it to Bianca, who couldn't get away from the Bobcat guarding her. The Bobcat slapped the ball away, but I recovered it and took it in for a layup. Nighthawks 7, Bobcats 2.

The Bobcats scored twice more in the first quarter, and both Bianca and Avery scored. So the quarter ended with us up 11–6, and Coach put me and Avery on the bench and rotated in Dina and Natalie. The rules of the league meant that no player could play all four quarters, so I figured she was taking me out now while we were ahead, and saving me for later so we could finish out strong.

Bianca played center in the second quarter, and she got the tip-off even though she was shorter than the Bobcats' center. We didn't turn it into points, though, because one of the Bobcats intercepted a pass between Tiff and Natalie.

I watched the game from the bench. Tiff was still on number 27, and she would not let that girl score! She was playing amazing defense. Even so, the Bobcats scored six points, and we only scored three—Natalie made a basket, and Tiff got a free throw when 27 fouled her with an elbow.

The second half started with the Nighthawks up 14–12. Coach gave us a half-time pep talk.

"Elle, go back in there and do what you did in the

first quarter," she said. "Keep making those confident shots. Their defense is getting more aggressive, so I want everybody to consider all your options carefully before passing, okay? Think before you throw."

"Yes, Coach!" we replied.

I felt totally energized as I ran back onto the court for the third quarter. Coach sat out Bianca, but she put in Avery, Amanda, Tiff, and Hannah.

I passed the ball to Amanda, and she passed it to Avery. Avery passed it to Hannah, but one of the Bobcats took it from her.

Then the Bobcats passed it down from one player to the next, swiftly and with confidence, and scored to tie up the game. Then Avery passed it to Hannah, who dribbled down the court and then passed it to me. Two Bobcats swarmed me, including the girl with the long braid, and I passed to Amanda, who was open right under the basket. She aimed but didn't make the shot.

Bobcats got control of the ball and took it down the court. One of the players passed to the long-braid girl, number 5, and I immediately ran to block her.

"Out of my way, Big Bird," the girl snarled, and I froze for a millisecond. She pivoted and took a shot, and the ball swished through the basket. Now the Bobcats were up 16–14.

I didn't have a lot of time to process number 5's trash talk—calling me "Big Bird" was pretty silly, but it still stung. Then I heard Blake's voice inside my head, telling me to toughen up. So when we had control of the ball again and I caught a pass from Tiff, I tore down the court like I had rockets in my shoes. I blew past all their defenders and made a sweet layup.

"Go, Elle!" I could hear cheers from the stands—Grandma and Pete were the loudest. But I didn't relax. My basket had tied up the score, 16–16, but I still had more work to do.

I tore down the court as the Bobcats tried to get back in the lead. Number 5 had the ball, and she passed it to her teammate, who took a shot from the three-point zone—and made it. Bobcats 19, Nighthawks 16.

Hannah threw the ball in to Tiff, who passed it sideways to me. Perfect. I took a shot from the three-point zone and tied up the game, 19–19.

"Keep up the pressure on the Bobcats out there!" Coach Ramirez told us. "They are hungry for this win. Don't let them get it!"

My heart was pounding as we went into the fourth quarter. The ref's whistle blew, and I ran back in with Caroline, Bianca, and Patrice. I faced number 5.

Big Bird, she mouthed, so the ref wouldn't hear her, and I just glared back at her. Then Avery threw the ball to Bianca.

Bianca took it down the court and passed it to Patrice. One of the Bobcats started shoving into Patrice with her shoulders in an attempt to get the ball. The ref blew his whistle, and Patrice got to take a foul shot. She sank it in for a point. Now it was Nighthawks 20, Bobcats 19.

From that point on, the game moved faster than any game I had ever played. The Bobcats scored. Then Bianca made a basket. The Bobcats scored again. Then Caroline got a knee from one of the Bobcats and got a foul shot.

As the clock wound down, the Bobcats scored again. Now the score was Bobcats 26, Nighthawks 23.

I thought of number 5 mouthing "Big Bird" to me and I knew that the Bobcats couldn't win. They didn't deserve to win. And I wasn't going to let them.

I got open for a pass and Bianca threw the ball to me. I took it down the court for another layup, zigzagging past the Bobcats defenders with so much control that I surprised even myself. Those ball-handling drills were paying off! Nighthawks 25, Bobcats 26.

"That's the Elle I want to see!" Coach called from the sidelines.

But I wasn't done. With twenty seconds on the clock, I jumped up to intercept a pass between the Bobcats. I caught it and then dribbled down the court. Number 5 ran up to me, blocking my path.

Now, number 5 might have been fast. She might have been a trash talker. But she was at least eight inches shorter than me.

I jumped up and took a shot. There's no way she could block me.

Swish!

The ref's whistle blew.

"Game over! Nighthawks win!"

We'd won the game 27–26. I smiled at number 5.

"Big Bird just beat you," I said.

No Fun

Number 5's face fell, and she ran to join her team. For a split second I felt bad about my comment. Had I stooped to her level? But then my teammates surrounded me whooping and cheering, and I started cheering too. We had won!

We lined up to slap hands with the Bobcats, and I noticed that number 5 avoided my eyes. Then we ran back to the bleachers to talk to our friends and families, and make plans for a postgame celebration.

Grandma hugged me so hard that I couldn't breathe. "Congratulations on your win, Elle!"

"You were great out there, Ellie! A real natural!" Grandpa said.

"Thanks," I said. "I'm glad you guys came."

"I'm very proud of you, Elle," Mom said. "Those Bobcats were playing very rough, though. I did not like to see that."

Before I could respond, my little cousins, Michael and Olivia, hugged my legs.

"You're so good, Elle!" Michael said.

"When I grow up, I want to be tall like you," said Olivia.

Uncle Danny grinned. "We'd better get a UConn scout to your next game, Elle. You were fantastic!"

Why is he bringing up UConn again? I wondered, but before the thought of moving far away from my family could bring me down, Amanda grabbed my arm.

"We're going to Sal's Pizza," she said. "My mom's driving."

I looked at my mom. "Can I go?" I felt guilty asking, because I knew the whole family had planned to go out for a late lunch after the game. But I was pumped up, and wanted to celebrate with my teammates.

"Of course," she said. "Do you need us to pick you up?"

"My mom can bring her home," Amanda said. "It's on the way."

I hugged everyone again, and a little while later the Nighthawks were sitting at a table in Sal's Pizzeria, splitting two plain pies and two with pepperoni.

"Those Bobcats were nasty," Avery said. "First with those negative chants, and then those fouls."

"They *really* wanted to win," Hannah remarked.

"But they didn't," Amanda said. "Thanks to Elle!"

I blushed. "We all played great," I said. "And anyway, I got really mad when that one girl called me Big Bird."

"What?!" Avery shrieked. "Why didn't you say something?"

I shrugged. "It's no big deal. It's dumb."

Bianca was cracking up. "Big Bird? That is hilarious."

"Come on, Bianca," Tiff said. "That's not funny."

"It's not nice, but you have to admit it's funny," she said. She looked around. "Right?"

Nobody answered her. Bianca shrugged. "Whatever," she said, and then she took a bite of her pizza.

Everybody started talking again, going over the big plays in the game, but I didn't join in. I wasn't upset about the Big Bird thing. I was deep in thought.

I had played a great game. We'd won. Everybody had cheered me and hugged me and praised me.

And while all that stuff was great, I realized that I hadn't had any fun. I had been worried about not messing up the whole game. And even though I'd played well, my playing was fueled by anger at the Bobcats. That definitely fueled my adrenaline while I was playing, but it wasn't a great feeling.

Was basketball supposed to be fun? I wondered. *Maybe not. Maybe it* is *just about winning.*

When we finished eating, Amanda's mom drove me, Avery, and Amanda home. We dropped off Avery first.

"Amanda tells me you have a very big dog," Mrs. O'Connor said as we headed to our neighborhood near the park in Greenmont.

"Zobe," I replied. "He's a Great Dane."

"He's so sweet, Mom," Amanda said. "And he and Freckles get along really well."

Amanda smiled at me from the front seat, and I smiled back. I felt myself blushing, and I wasn't sure I knew why.

"See you tomorrow!" Amanda said as I got out of the car.

"Yeah, see you!" I said. "Thanks for the ride!"

Maybe basketball had stopped being fun. But without basketball, I never would have become friends with Amanda, I realized. And maybe we wouldn't be friends anymore if I stopped playing.

Why couldn't basketball be as much fun on the court as it is off the court? I wondered.

The next morning, I headed straight to Tiff's locker after Mom dropped me off. The night before, I'd finally baked some oatmeal–chocolate chip cookies for her. I'd put them in a paper bag and then wrote, *For Tiff—the Ultimate Cookie. From Elle*, on the front in marker.

I was waiting for Tiff when Bianca approached.

She glanced at the bag and raised her eyebrows.

"What are you trying to do?" she asked.

"What do you mean?" I replied. "I'm just giving Tiff some cookies to thank her for helping me study."

"So you're trying to steal my best friend?" Bianca asked.

I was shocked—and then I realized that Bianca's competitive nature probably meant that *everything* was competition to her. Even friendship.

"No, I'm just being nice," I said. "And if you want to talk about stealing friends, what about Blake?"

"That's different," Bianca said. "You don't like Blake the way I like him."

"Why does that make a difference?" I asked. "He's one of my best friends!"

That's when Tiff walked up. She looked surprised to see Bianca and me talking.

"Hey," she said. "What's going on?"

I handed her the bag. "I baked you those cookies we talked about," I said.

"Wow, thank you!" Tiff said, smiling at me. She dipped into the bag. "Is it wrong to eat one now?"

"I think it's fine," I said. "They do have oatmeal in them. So it's kind of like breakfast, right?"

Next to me, Bianca was silently fuming.

Tiff held up a cookie. "Do you want one?" she asked Bianca.

"No, thanks," Bianca said, and then she walked off.

Tiff looked at me. "What happened there?"

The whole exchange with Bianca had been so awkward that I didn't feel like explaining it.

"Nothing," I said. "See you in class!"

I headed to my locker, thinking about the conversation with Bianca.

She's one of the reasons why basketball isn't fun anymore, I thought. And I had no idea how to fix that problem.

What Now?

That was a close game yesterday," Coach Ramirez told us as we sat in the bleachers that afternoon. "Let's take a few minutes to see what went wrong."

For once I wasn't nervous about the video review. I knew I had played a great game.

Coach paused at Patrice's missed shot in the first quarter. Then she paused when a Bobcat swatted the ball away from Bianca and explained that Bianca could have pivoted to avoid that. In the second quarter she stopped to compliment Tiff's defense and criticize Natalie for her footwork.

When the third quarter began, I was hopeful that Coach was going to praise me for all of the baskets I made. Instead she paused when I passed the ball to Amanda.

"Elle, you've done this before," she said. "You passed to Amanda, but Tiff was in a better position to shoot. That decision cost us two points."

My stomach dropped. "Yes, Coach."

Then she stopped again, when number 5 scored when I was guarding her. "Here's another two points you cost us, Elle," she said. "We've gone over that defensive drill a thousand times. You weren't in the right position."

"Sorry, Coach," I said, and I could feel my face getting red. It was like Coach was putting all the blame on me for the score being so tight!

Then Coach turned off the video. She didn't even show the fourth quarter, where I made those game-winning baskets.

"Okay, girls, let's warm up!" she said.

That is so unfair! I thought. I did my squat thrusts

with the rest of the team, but I felt miserable.

It bothered me so much that when practice was over, I hung back and asked to talk to Coach. I figured I had nothing to lose.

"What is it, Elle?" Coach asked.

"It's just . . ." I almost lost my nerve, but I pressed on. "I was just wondering why you didn't, you know, talk about the baskets I made to win the game. You only pointed out when I messed up."

"Well, if you hadn't made those moves, you might not have had to make those game-winning baskets," Coach replied.

I pressed on. "But it wasn't just me making mistakes!" I said. "I feel like you're singling me out when you do the replays."

"Well, you're right," Coach said. "I do single you out. You've got great potential, Elle, and it's my job as your coach to push you to get there."

"Great potential?" I asked. "You mean because of my height?"

"Of course," Coach said. "But also because you're a great shooter. That's a winning combination.

Listen, this is an important time in your journey as a basketball player, Elle. If I just let you roam the court and shoot, I wouldn't be doing you any favors. I need to craft you into a well-rounded player. That's what's going to serve you in high school and beyond."

My head was spinning. There it was again—the assumption that I wanted to play basketball for the rest of my life. The idea that my height was determining my destiny.

"Got it, Coach," I said. "Thanks."

I walked to the locker room, and Patrice passed me and nodded her head. I realized that she'd been more quiet than usual, ever since that day she'd left the gym in tears. She didn't look happy about playing basketball either.

Patrice probably has to keep playing, I guessed, *because her mom is the coach.*

But maybe I don't have to . . .

Do your homework between 7 p.m. and 9 p.m. tonight, Elle!

The phone flashed me a reminder as I walked

into the house. Amanda's mom had dropped me off, and the kitchen smelled like chicken soup.

I knew I had to do homework that night, but it was only 5:30, thankfully. I found Mom and Beth in the kitchen.

"How was practice?" Mom asked.

"Fine," I replied, and I greeted Beth.

Love you, I signed into her palm. I hadn't been spending as much time with Beth as I'd wanted to these last few weeks. My new schedule included plenty of free time, but I wasn't spending enough of it with Beth. And that made me feel sad.

Love you, she signed back, and I held her hand and leaned my head on her shoulder.

Mom sat down next to me. "Soup's in the slow cooker, so I've got some time," she said. "And you look like you need to talk."

I took a deep breath before I began. This wasn't going to be easy.

"I've been thinking a lot about basketball," I told her. "And about . . . whether I was born to play, like everybody says I am."

Mom nodded. "Yes, people do say that a lot."

"They mainly say that because I'm tall," I said. "But what if I was short? I might have a whole different life right now."

"That's an interesting way of looking at it," Mom said. "I suppose that could be true. So are you saying you wish you were short?"

I frowned. "Not exactly," I replied. "I sometimes wish I wasn't so tall. Just regular tall. But I guess I mean that if I had been short, maybe I would have had a chance to do different things besides basketball."

"I see," Mom said.

"And the thing is, I'm not sure if I'm supposed to be playing basketball," I went on. "But I feel like everybody's counting on me to do it. You and Dad. Grandma and Grandpa. My friends. If I . . . if I quit, I will let everyone down."

Mom reached out and grasped my hand. "Elle, the only way you would ever disappoint your dad and me is if you quit something without giving it your best try. We know you've put a lot of effort into basketball. If you decide you don't want to play, well, that's your decision. I just hope you would find another activity you like because I think it's important for kids to be involved in something. I wouldn't want to see you lying around playing video games all day."

I laughed. "Mom, the only video games I play are basketball games, and I don't even play them that much."

"You know what I mean," Mom said. "I would hate to see you turn into a couch potato."

"That would not happen," I said. "But I can't quit, because Avery would never forgive me anyway."

"Are you sure about that?" Mom asked. "You have known Avery for a very long time. Is she that kind of person?"

I thought about Avery, and how she was one of the most understanding people I had ever met.

I shook my head. "No, I guess not. But everything would change anyway. It would be too weird to know everybody was practicing and hanging out without me. I would miss them too much."

"I can't make this decision for you, Elle," she said. "Just promise me that you will think it through.

And whatever you decide, your dad and I will support you."

I leaned over and hugged her.

"Thanks, Mom," I said.

Then my phone flashed with a notification from U-Plan.

Elle, tonight you have study time between 7 p.m. and 9 p.m.!

I groaned. The app was still glitching, giving me notifications when I didn't want them.

It was annoying. I knew the app was helping me plan my routine, but why couldn't it help me with more important stuff too?

Quit basketball at 3:15 p.m. today, Elle! You will have more time to try other things!

Don't quit basketball at 3:15 p.m. today, Elle! You will miss spending time with Avery, Amanda, and all your other teammates!

That would make things so much easier! But unfortunately, the U-Plan app could not help me. I had to decide for myself.

My Fast Break

On Wednesday morning I still hadn't decided what I was going to do. And when I got to school, my decision became even harder.

There was a poster up in the hallway next to the main office, with an image of two hands, one orange and one blue, reaching out toward each other with a red heart between them. The sign read:

JOIN THE BUDDY CLUB!

SPRING MEADOW'S FIRST ANTI-BULLYING CLUB

MEETS WEDNESDAYS AT 3 P.M.

ADVISOR: MS. EBEAR

I stopped in my tracks. An anti-bullying club sounded awesome! I loved the idea of making the world a friendlier place. And Ms. Ebear was my favorite teacher! Of course, I had basketball practice every Wednesday after school. Although I'd have Wednesdays free when practice was over, but in the spring I usually joined the travel team, and last year I'd had Wednesday practices for that, too.

It's a sign, I thought. *I'm supposed to quit basketball and join the Anti-Bullying Club!*

And then I thought of something else. *I might even be able to join the volleyball team, too!*

Avery ran up to me. I was about to tell her about the new club, but she started talking first.

"Do you think Coach will be hard on us at practice today?" she asked.

I shrugged. "Probably."

Avery sighed. "You know, Elle, it's been pretty stressful being on the team these days," she said. "I'm so glad we're on the team together. It makes it a lot more fun."

It was almost like Avery knew I was thinking of

quitting, and she had said the perfect thing to get me to stay. But she couldn't have known that, could she?

"Yeah," I agreed. "I'm glad you're on the team too."

An imaginary U-Plan notification flashed in my head.

Do not quit the team today at 3:15 p.m.!

So I didn't. I played through practice like I had been doing, staying as focused as I could and doing my best. We did the same drills as always, and Coach Ramirez didn't work us any harder than usual.

But on Friday, she was on fire again.

"So, I want to get this team ready to start learning some fast-break strategies," Coach said after we had warmed up. "But first I think we need to improve our passing game, so we're going to do some passing drills."

Amanda raised her hand. "Coach, what's a fast-break strategy?"

"It just means that when we're on offense, we get the ball into a scoring position as quickly as possible, leaving the defense in our dust," Coach replied. "But we can't even think about fast breaks until we improve our passing. So let's divide into two teams."

She split us up into our usual scrimmage teams. Me, Avery, Dina, Hannah, and Caroline against Bianca, Tiff, Amanda, Patrice, and Natalie.

"Elle's team, you're on offense first," Coach said. "And this drill calls for one-on-one defense. Bianca, you're on Elle. Tiff is on Avery. Amanda's on Caroline. Dina, you take Patrice. And Natalie, you've got Hannah."

Then she positioned us all on the court. Natalie and Hannah on the left side of the basket, Dina and Patrice on the right side, Amanda and Caroline on the right side of the three-point line, and the rest of us in the free throw lane.

"This drill is about passing, not shooting," Coach explained. "Elle's team, your objective is to pass the ball to one another without Bianca's team stealing or deflecting the ball. If the ball goes out of bounds, you're done. There is no dribbling or shooting allowed. If your team can make ten successful passes, you score one point. Does everybody get it?"

"Yes, Coach!" we answered.

Coach tossed me the ball. I had the advantage going first, because Bianca wasn't ready to defend me. I passed the ball low to Caroline. Amanda lunged for it, but Caroline caught it.

"Remember your strategies, Caroline!" Coach called out.

Caroline faked left, then faked right, then quickly moved left and shot the ball over to Hannah.

"Two passes!" Coach called out. "Keep it going, offense!"

Hannah quickly passed to Avery, and she passed it to Patrice. But Dina swatted the ball away from Patrice before she could catch it.

"Only four passes, Elle's team," Coach said. "You'll have to do better next time."

I shook my head. This was going to be harder than I'd thought!

Bianca's team only made five passes when it was

their turn, so I didn't feel as bad. It took both teams a few rounds to get the hang of it. Our team got to ten passes first.

"Finally!" Coach said. "One point for Elle's team!"

It would have been kind of fun if Coach hadn't started riding me.

"Elle, use your height to your advantage! Hold that ball above your head where Bianca can't get it!"

"Elle, why did you pass to Avery when she wasn't open?"

"Elle, pivot!"

"Elle!"

"Elle!

"Elle!"

That's all I heard, anyway. Coach calling me out over and over again.

Then Patrice passed me the ball. I held it up over my head, and Bianca jumped up and tapped it right out of my hands before I could get a grip on it. I jogged to retrieve it as it bounced away.

"Yes!" Bianca cheered. "Coach, come on! I can do it! I can play center!"

Something snapped inside me at that moment. A few things became crystal clear.

Bianca was never going to stop giving me a hard time about being center.

Coach was never going to stop singling me out.

It was too much!

I passed Bianca the ball.

"Go for it," I said, passing her the ball. "I think I need a break."

With my hands shaking, I walked out of bounds.

"Elle, where are you going?" Avery called out.

I didn't answer her. I ran into the locker room and grabbed my duffel bag. Then I ran out of the gym as fast as I could, my face burning.

I texted my mom. **Please come get me now!**

Sure. You ok?

I quit, I texted back.

I'll be there as soon as I can, Mom replied.

I walked to the main entrance and stepped outside to wait. The chilly air felt good on my face. My heart was pounding.

Had I done the right thing?

What Have I Done?

Elle! Are you okay?"

Avery's face looked worried and sympathetic on my laptop screen—not angry, as I had feared.

"Yeah," I said. "I'm sorry, Avery. I just don't want to play anymore. I really thought about it."

Avery nodded. "I know you haven't been happy. Everybody can see it. What did your parents say?"

"They were pretty cool about it," I replied. "I'd already told Mom I was thinking about it, and she said the decision was up to me. Dad was more disappointed, I think, but he said he understood. Coach is talking to Mom on the phone now, but I don't think it will do any good. I'm not going back."

Saying it out loud like that, I knew I meant it. It felt scary and good at the same time.

"Yeah, you sound like you've made up your mind," Avery said.

"Mom wants me to write a letter to Coach, formally resigning," I told her. "So I guess when I do that it will be official."

Then I asked the question I was dreading. "Is everybody mad at me?"

"Nobody's mad," Avery replied. "And I even think Bianca feels bad."

"Really?" I asked. "I figured she'd be thrilled about it."

Avery shook her head. "No, she seemed pretty freaked out. I think she's worried that it's going to hurt the team," she explained. "Natalie wants to decorate your locker with positive messages on Monday to convince you to come back, but I said I didn't think you wanted that. That we should let you figure it out first."

"Thanks," I replied, feeling relieved. The last thing I wanted was for everybody to make a big deal out of my leaving the team.

"So, I was calling to see if you want to go to the mall tomorrow," Avery said.

"I have obedience class with Zobe," I told her.

"How about after?" she asked.

I looked at my phone. "Sure," I said. "And then you need to help me fix my U-Plan. I'm going to need to change my schedule."

"Yeah, I guess so," Avery said, and she sounded a little sad. "I'll ask my mom to drive us to the mall. I'll pick you up at one o'clock. Okay?"

"Okay," I replied, and then I signed off. As I did, my phone started blowing up with texts.

From Natalie: Elle, noooooooooo!

From Caroline: We'll miss you!

From Tiff: We will always be your team-mates!

From Amanda: Hope you are ok, Elle. And

hope we can still hang out .

The texts made me feel good and bad at the same time. Good because nobody was angry with me. And bad because I was no longer part of the Nighthawks. Being part of a team was the best thing about playing basketball, and I knew I would miss it.

I leaned over to Zobe and buried my face in his fur. I picked up my head to ask, "Did I do the right thing, Zobe?"

He looked at me, and then he answered me with the funniest noise. Not a bark, not a whine, but somewhere in between.

Aaaroooo?

It was almost like he was saying, "I don't know." I laughed.

"I don't know either, Zobe."

Colonial Mall was crazy crowded the next day because everyone was doing their holiday shopping. The place is huge, with four floors, restaurants, a food court, and a movie theater, but every floor was packed with people.

"So why are we here again?" I asked as a mom pushing a stroller accidentally bumped into me.

"Because I like the mall," Avery said. "And I need to find a present for my grandparents."

We were walking past Sports Locker and she stopped. "Do you want to go in and check out the new shoes?"

I stopped. Normally I would have raced inside. But I wasn't playing basketball anymore. Did it make sense for me to still be obsessed with basketball shoes?

"Um . . ." I stood there, not sure what to say.

"Hey, is that Blake?" Avery asked, pointing into the shop.

Blake was inside Sports Locker, looking at boys' basketball shoes.

Avery headed in to say hi, and I followed, a little nervously. Blake and I hadn't really talked to each other since I'd given him a hard time about Bianca.

"Oh, hey, Avery. Hey, Elle," he said.

"Getting new shoes?" I asked.

Blake shrugged. "Just looking. I need to, um,

find a birthday present for Bianca. But I don't even know where to look. So I just came here."

"We can help you," Avery said. "There's a really cute accessories shop on the second floor. Right, Elle?"

I wasn't exactly thrilled to be helping Blake buy a present for Bianca, but it felt good to be with my two best friends again. I nodded. Blake followed us out of Sports Locker, and we walked in awkward silence to the escalators. I didn't like that at all. Blake and Avery were my two best friends in the world. I didn't want that to change.

"Blake, I'm sorry," I said. "I didn't mean to give you a hard time about Bianca. It's your life. You can do what you want."

"It's cool," Blake said. "And I'm sorry too. I heard you quit the team. Is it because of Bianca?"

I shook my head. "That's only part of it," I said. "I have a lot of reasons."

Avery, sensing how hard this was for me, sniffed the air. "Pretzel Barn!" she cried.

Pretzel Barn made the best hot pretzels on the

East Coast. Even my grandpa thought so, and he's from Philly. Whenever Avery, Blake, and I go to the mall, we always get pretzels from there.

"I think I would be much more equipped to pick out a gift if I had a hot pretzel in my belly," Blake said, and Avery and I laughed.

"Of course," I said. "What kind of dip should we get? Hot mustard?"

"Nacho!" Avery said.

"No way. Honey mustard," Blake said.

As we headed to the second floor I realized that I felt happier and more relaxed than I had in weeks, although I still wasn't sure if I had made the right decision. Would I miss playing basketball? What kind of person would the non-basketball-playing Elle turn out to be?

I wasn't sure—but I knew I wanted to find out.

In my dream I was tearing down the basketball court, dribbling so fast past the defenders that they were just a blur. The crowd chanted my name. "Elle! Elle! Elle! Elle!"

I approached the basket and jumped up, my body feeling light as I floated upward, ready to dunk. I flew high above the basket, but when I looked down, I didn't see net. I saw a dark, swirling tunnel of wind.

"Nooooooo!" I yelled as the tunnel sucked me inside. My body twisted and turned as I plummeted down into the tunnel, about to . . .

"Zobe, no!" I cried. My Great Dane was licking my face as I sprang awake, my heart pounding from the dream.

I thought I knew what the dream meant. On Friday I had quit the school basketball team. Today was Monday, and I'd have to face most of my teammates for the first time since I'd walked out. I was pretty nervous about that.

I pulled my covers over my head. Zobe nudged them aside with his big doggy nose. I knew he wanted his morning walk, and breakfast.

"Can't we just stay home today, Zobe?" I asked him. "Let's just stay right here in this bed."

"Woof!" Zobe gave a loud, deep bark. I sighed and threw off the covers. Zobe was not going to let me win this argument.

Twenty minutes later Zobe was eating his kibble and I was eating my cereal, nervously tapping my foot on the floor.

Mom sat down next to me and plunked her steaming coffee mug on the table. "Jim's going to drive you and Blake to school this week. I'll be picking you both up, except on days when Blake has basketball practice, or when you're staying late for the anti-bully club, or Camp Cooperation. Then I'll just get you."

I nodded. Jim is my older brother, Blake is one of my best friends, and we all go to Spring Meadow, a private school in Wilmington, Delaware. We live in Greenmont, which is about thirty minutes away. And now that Jim is a senior, and has his own car, he helps out sometimes.

"What am I doing?" Jim asked, yawning as he walked into the kitchen.

"I believe you are driving Elle and Blake to school," Dad said, not looking up from his laptop. He owns a real-estate business in Wilmington, and he works a lot. Even during breakfast!

"Cool," Jim said, and I felt grateful that he wasn't the kind of older brother who would complain about taking his little sister to school.

Actually, I'm not sure if the phrase "little sister" can technically apply to me. I'm twelve years old and six feet tall. So I'm not very little. It's one of the reasons I started playing basketball in the first place.

It's also one of the reasons I quit.

Jim grabbed a protein bar from the cabinet. "You ready, Elle?"

I jumped up from my seat. "Yes!" I put my dishes in the sink and then moved over to my sister, Beth, who was sitting in her wheelchair at the end of the table.

I leaned over and let Beth sniff my head so she would know it was me, because she couldn't see or hear me. Then I took her hand and traced two symbols onto her palm with my finger, part of the special language that we used to communicate with her.

Good-bye. Love.

Beth took my hand and answered me. *Love.*

"I'll be at the pickup area at three," Mom told me.

"Thanks," I said, and inside I was thinking, *Three, not five, because I'm not going to basketball practice. Weird!* I was going to have to get used to my new Monday routine.

I walked outside with Jim and saw Blake making a beeline for Jim's car in the driveway.

"Shotgun!" I yelled, and dashed to the front passenger seat side of the car.

"Not fair!" Blake protested.

"Of course it's fair," I said. "I called it."

Blake couldn't argue with that. Those shotgun rules had a history going back to when we had both grown tall enough to sit in the front seat. He frowned and slid into the back. I got into the passenger side and then, to bust him, I pushed the seat back as far as it would go.

"Hey, now that's definitely not fair!" Blake cried.

Jim shook his head. "Are you two twelve or five?" he asked.

I quickly pulled up my seat and locked in my seat belt. I heard Blake yawn behind me.

"I hate Mondays," he complained as Jim pulled the car out of the driveway.

"I hate *this* Monday," I said. "I haven't seen anybody since I quit the team, except for you and Avery."

Avery is my other best friend. She and I played on the girls' basketball team together, the Nighthawks. Pretty much everybody I hang out with in school is on the team.

"You think it will be a big deal?" my brother asked.

"I *know* it will," I groaned.

"You might be right," Blake said. "Bianca's been texting me all weekend, freaking out."

"Really?" I asked. "I thought she'd be thrilled. She hated it when Coach Ramirez made me center."

"Well, she's happy she's center," Blake admitted, "but she's worried about the team. She wants to make it to the championships. And she doesn't think the Nighthawks can get there without you."

"Of course they can," I said quickly, but that was followed by a pang of doubt. I hadn't really thought about the fact that my leaving could hurt the team's record. That they might lose without me.

They won't, I told myself. *They've got too many good players.* Bianca was really good. So was Avery, and Tiff and Dina were pretty solid. They didn't need me.

That didn't stop me from feeling guilty though, especially when we got to school and my friends Hannah and Natalie ambushed me at my locker. They both squashed me in a double hug.

"Elle, please don't quit!" cried pink-haired Natalie

as they pulled away from me. "I thought you loved basketball more than any of us!"

"I still love basketball," I said. "I just don't feel comfortable playing it competitively right now."

"What can we do to get you to stay?" Hannah asked. I felt awful, because her big brown eyes looked so sad when she said it.

"Nothing," I said. "I mean, thanks, but this is just something I need to do. It's not personal."

Hannah sighed. "I thought you would say that."

"I get it," Natalie added. "As long as you're happy, Elle."

"Thanks," I replied, although I wasn't sure if I was happy, exactly. Relieved, maybe. But I hadn't gotten to "happy" yet.

Next, Bianca walked by with her best friend, Tiff. Bianca didn't say a word to me; she just tossed her glossy black hair as she passed and glared at me. Tiff, who was wearing a blue hijab over her dark brown hair, shot me a look of apology.

Luckily, Avery was right behind them. She stopped and grabbed my arm.

"You all right?" she asked.

I nodded. "Just walk with me to homeroom, okay?"

"Sure," Avery said.

I'm glad I asked her, because even though it was a short walk, I passed all the rest of my teammates.

"You can't *really* be quitting, Elle," Dina said, talking fast as she kept pace with us. "Say it's not true."

"It's true," I replied, and Dina stopped following us and shook her head.

Patrice looked up at me from her locker and just nodded. The coach's daughter, she had almost quit too, a week ago. She kind of looked like she wanted to talk to me, but she didn't say anything.

Then Caroline walked up to me and Avery.

"I'm going to miss you on the team, Elle," she said.

"Yeah, me too," I said. "But I'll still see you at Camp Cooperation!"

Caroline and I both volunteer for this after-school program for kids with special needs.

Then Avery turned the corner and literally bumped into the last (but definitely not least) member of the team, Amanda. She smiled at me, and I smiled back. But seeing Amanda always makes me smile.

"Hey, guys," she said. "Elle, I mean it. We need to go on a doggy date this weekend."

I laughed. "I definitely want to," I said. Amanda has a dog too—an English springer spaniel named Freckles. "I just need to check my scheduling app. Even without basketball, I still seem to have a packed schedule."

"Make sure to squeeze me in," Amanda said with a grin, and then we all stepped into homeroom together and took our seats as the bell rang.

"Good morning, Spring Meadow students and staff!" Principal Lubin's morning voice, always cheerful, rang out over the school sound system. "I'm wearing my sunglasses to school today and do you know why? Because the students here at Spring Meadow are so bright!"

Everybody in class groaned. Principal Lubin's puns were always painful, but he was a really nice principal, so we all forgave him for it.

"I'm proud to reannounce that Ms. Ebear is organizing the Buddy Club, an anti-bullying club in the middle school that will meet after school on Wednesdays," he said. "This club is open to all students in grades six through eight. We're currently working on a club for elementary school students that will meet during lunch period. Stay tuned for more details, and if you haven't already, look for the sign-up sheet for Ms. Ebear's club in the middle school front hallway."

Then we said the Pledge of Allegiance, and the speaker crackled off. Besides being the advisor for the anti-bullying club, Ms. Ebear was also our homeroom and World History teacher, and my favorite. She wore her shiny brown hair in a neat bob, and she had kind green eyes behind her severe black eyeglasses.

"I need to thank Principal Lubin for that shout-out," she said. "And I hope to see some of you in this class at our meeting on Wednesday."

Avery leaned toward me. "I wish I could go, but we—I mean, I—have basketball practice."

I nodded, feeling guilty. I was planning to join Ms. Ebear's club. In fact, learning about it was one of the reasons I had decided to quit basketball. Avery had been really supportive of my decision to quit, but I felt bad telling her that I was joining the club when I knew she couldn't—so I didn't say anything.

After homeroom I stayed in the room for World History class with Ms. Ebear. Nobody talked to me about quitting the basketball team, which was a relief. Same in second period science class. But then came third period gym.

I had changed into my green gym shirt and shorts and was leaving the locker room when Kenya and Maggie approached me. I know them because Spring Meadow is a small school, but I've never really hung out with them. They were both athletic—and both on the girls' volleyball team.

"I heard you quit basketball," Kenya said.

"Yeah," I replied. Where was this going?

"We need your help on the volleyball team," Kenya continued. "Lauren sprained her wrist and we're down a player until she gets better. And we've seen you play in gym and we know you're good."

Maggie hadn't said anything yet—I knew she

was quiet—but she stared at me with intense blue eyes that peered out from under her blond bangs.

"Oh wow, I don't know what to say," I replied. "I mean, I like volleyball. But I . . . when are the practices?"

"Tuesdays after school, and Fridays at five," Kenya replied. "And then a game every Friday at seven."

I bit my lip, thinking. The schedule was definitely less stressful than the basketball schedule. It still left me free to volunteer on Thursdays, and to join Ms. Ebear's club. I had loved playing volleyball in gym class. And it would only be temporary, until Lauren's wrist healed. Still . . .

"I need to think about it," I said.

"Don't think too hard," Kenya told me. "If you decide to do it, come to practice tomorrow."

I nodded. "Okay," I said.

Avery walked up to me. "What was that about?" she asked.

"Oh, nothing," I said. Once again, I felt awkward telling Avery I might be doing something cool instead of basketball. Avery looked at me suspiciously, but she didn't press me.

I thought about Kenya's offer as I jogged around the gym. One reason I had quit basketball was because it was getting stressful. Coach Ramirez expected a lot from me. Would volleyball be the same? I wondered.

I jogged past Bianca and Dina. Dina nodded to me, but Bianca deliberately looked the other way.

What was her deal? Bianca had been mad when Coach Ramirez had given me her position on the team, and the pressure and taunting I'd gotten from Bianca was another reason I'd quit. But even though I wasn't on the team anymore, nothing had gotten better. I'd thought maybe she'd be nicer to me once I left, but obviously I was wrong about that.

I glanced back at the volleyball girls. Was one of them another Bianca? Would I be walking from one bad situation into another?

That's not the only reason you quit, I reminded myself. One of the main reasons was because it felt like my height had sentenced me to play basketball . . . forever. People were already telling me that I was on a track to become a pro player, and I was only twelve! What if I wanted to do something different with my life? If I didn't find out now, when would I?

You love sports, I told myself. *Why not give volleyball a try?*

That question bounced around in my head all day. I decided to ask my parents about it at dinner, and when I did they were thrilled, which surprised me a little bit.

"I think it's a great idea to try something new!" Dad said.

Mom nodded. "I was worried that you were just going to be moping around, Elle. I know you're joining the anti-bullying club, but that's only one day a week, and basketball was such a big commitment."

"The volleyball schedule is easier," I said. "I can help out the team and still have time to try some new things."

"It seems like a good idea," Mom agreed. "But are you sure that you won't have the same issues with volleyball that you did with basketball? I hated seeing the way the pressure got to you, Elle."

I shrugged. "I have no idea, because I've never been on a volleyball team before. All I know is basketball. But I think maybe it's worth finding out. And the team needs me—I'd really be helping them out."

"Fair enough," Mom replied. "So have you decided?"

I took a deep breath. "Yeah. I'm going to do it."

"Great!" Mom said. "E-mail me your new practice and game schedule."

After dinner I saw I had a text on my phone from an unknown number. It was Kenya.

Got your number from Blake. Did you decide? We have practice tomorrow.

Wow, she's persistent, I thought. It was kind of flattering, though.

See you at practice, I typed back. **I'll join the team until Lauren is better!!**

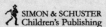